3 8002 02054 602 6

FIN

She suddenly couldn't help yearning to feel those sexy roller-coaster lips pressed to hers…

Would they be as soft and warm as they looked? As supple? What kind of kisser was he? Not pinch-lipped the way Wes sometimes was, she thought. Relaxed, confident, natural—that was Dag and probably how Dag kissed…

But that wasn't anything she should be thinking about!

She jerked her eyes away just about the time Dag said, more to himself than to her, "But you're engaged…to a Rumson…"

D0522641

Dear Reader,

It's Christmastime in Northbridge and there's no place Dag McKendrick would rather be. Family, friends, decorations, festivities and genuine goodwill toward everyone. It's home.

For Shannon Duffy it's something else. It's a place to spend the holiday with the biological brother who has come into her life after a year of losses. Losses that not only included her parents and her beloved grandmother, but also the end of her three-year-long relationship with a politician all of Montana thinks she's still engaged to.

Proximity—and the fact that Shannon is selling Dag her late grandmother's house—brings Shannon and Dag together. But Dag's dauntless high spirits are just what she needs. So like any Christmas treat, Shannon lets herself indulge a little. And then a little more. And then a little more.

But that's Christmas for you...

I hope yours is wonderful, and that the new year brings with it only the best of everything!

Happy, happy holidays!

Victoria Pade

THE BACHELOR'S CHRISTMAS BRIDE

BY
VICTORIA PADE

All the characters in this book have no existence outside the imagination of the author, and have no relation whatsoever to anyone bearing the same name or names. They are not even distantly inspired by any individual known or unknown to the author, and all the incidents are pure invention.

All Rights Reserved including the right of reproduction in whole or in part in any form. This edition is published by arrangement with Harlequin Enterprises II B.V./S.à.r.l. The text of this publication or any part thereof may not be reproduced or transmitted in any form or by any means, electronic or mechanical, including photocopying, recording, storage in an information retrieval system, or otherwise, without the written permission of the publisher.

This book is sold subject to the condition that it shall not, by way of trade or otherwise, be lent, resold, hired out or otherwise circulated without the prior consent of the publisher in any form of binding or cover other than that in which it is published and without a similar condition including this condition being imposed on the subsequent purchaser.

® and ™ are trademarks owned and used by the trademark owner and/or its licensee. Trademarks marked with ® are registered with the United Kingdom Patent Office and/or the Office for Harmonisation in the Internal Market and in other countries.

First published in Great Britain 2012
by Mills & Boon, an imprint of Harlequin (UK) Limited,
Eton House, 18-24 Paradise Road, Richmond, Surrey TW9 1SR

© Victoria Pade 2010

ISBN: 978 0 263 89482 0
ebook ISBN: 978 1 408 97867 2

23-1112

Harlequin (UK) policy is to use papers that are natural, renewable and recyclable products and made from wood grown in sustainable forests. The logging and manufacturing processes conform to the legal environmental regulations of the country of origin.

Printed and bound in Spain
by Blackprint CPI, Barcelona

Victoria Pade is a *USA TODAY* bestselling author of numerous romance novels. She has two beautiful and talented daughters—Cori and Erin—and is a native of Colorado, where she lives and writes. A devoted chocolate lover, she's in search of the perfect chocolate-chip cookie recipe. For information about her latest and upcoming releases, and to find recipes for some of the decadent desserts her characters enjoy, log on to www.vikkipade.com.

Coventry City Council	
CEN*	
3 8002 02054 602 6	
Askews & Holts	Jan-2013
ROM	£3.49
	291.13

Chapter One

"Ho! Ho! Ho! What good skaters you are!"

Shannon Duffy smiled a little at what she saw and heard in the distance when she got out of her car.

After a long drive from Billings, she'd just arrived in the small town of Northbridge, Montana. At the end of Main Street, she'd spotted a parking space near the town square and pulled into it so she could get out and stretch for a minute.

Not far from the parking area was an open-air ice skating rink and it was there that a group of preschool-age children were apparently being taught—by Santa Claus—how to skate. Or at least they were being taught by a man dressed in a Santa suit, using the *ho-ho-hos* to encourage them.

Christmas was a little more than a week away and Shannon was anything but sorry to have it herald the close of the past year. It had been a rough year for her.

Very rough…

But as she breathed in the cold, clear air of the country town, as she watched the joy of kids slip-sliding around the ice rink that was surrounded by a pine-bough-and-red-ribbon-adorned railing, she was glad she'd come. She already felt just a tiny bit less disconnected than she had, just a tiny bit less alone, almost as if the small town her late grandmother had loved was holding out its arms to welcome her.

Shannon had suffered three losses this year. Four, if she counted Wes.

She'd lost her dad at the beginning of January, and her mom just three months after that. Their deaths hadn't come as a surprise; both of her parents had been ill most of their lives. But when, in August, her grandmother had suddenly and unexpectedly had a heart attack and died, too, that had been a shock. And it had meant that her entire family was gone in just a matter of months.

Then her relationship with Wes Rumson had ended on top of it all.…

But now her trip to Northbridge was twofold. Primarily, she was there to attend the wedding of and spend the holiday with the people she'd come to think of as her New Wave of family.

Two months earlier she'd been contacted by a man named Chase Mackey. Out of the blue he'd made the announcement that he was one of three brothers and a sister she'd been separated from when she was barely eighteen months old, when they'd lost their parents to a car accident and—with no other family—had been put into the system and up for adoption.

Shannon had known that she was adopted. She just hadn't known—before Chase Mackey's call—that she had biological siblings out in the world.

And not even too far out in the world at that since Chase Mackey had been calling her from Northbridge where her grandmother had lived and owned the small farm that Shannon had inherited at the end of the summer.

The farm was the second reason she was in Northbridge. Today she was to attend the closing on the sale of the property that she had no inclination to keep.

"Ooh, Tim! You okay?"

One of the little boy skaters had fallen soundly on his rump and Shannon heard Santa's question as she watched him race impressively to the child, clearly not inhibited by the bulky red suit and what was obviously padding around his middle.

Tim was a trouper, though. He fought the tears that his puffed-out lower lip threatened, let Santa help him up and get him steadied on his feet again. Then, casting nothing but a glance in the direction of the adults who looked on from the sidelines, the child let Santa ease him back to the group without making a bigger deal of the fall than it had called for.

Shannon silently approved of how the whole thing had played out.

Not that she had any reason to approve or disapprove, it was just that she was missing her job and some of that kicked in as she watched the scene.

She'd taught kindergarten since she'd graduated from college. It was a job she loved, but she was currently on sabbatical. Her grandmother's death had just been one blow too many and she'd needed to take some time.

It was a job she loved but might not be going back to. At least not exactly the way she'd done it before, not if she accepted her old friend's offer and moved to Beverly Hills instead....

But that possibility was in the mulling stages and for the next week and two days she was just going to get to know her new brother, and her new nephew, and try to enjoy this first holiday without the only family she'd ever known.

She looked away from Santa and the skaters and took her cell phone from her coat pocket. She'd lost service just before getting to Northbridge and she wondered if she was back within range or if she was going to have a problem while she was here.

No problem, she had service again.

And a message…

The message was from Wes's secretary, informing her that Wes wanted to know when she arrived safely at her destination.

Shannon appreciated the concern the same way she'd appreciated it when Wes had inquired about her plans for the holidays to make sure she wasn't spending them alone.

But merely the fact that it was Wes's secretary calling now rather than Wes himself was a glaring reminder of why she'd turned down the proposal of the man she'd been involved with for the last three years.

Wes Rumson. The Hope-For-The-Future of the Rumson family political machine that had provided a long history of Montana's district attorneys, senators, representatives, mayors and now—if Wes's campaign was successful—a governor.

The man who would have definitely provided her with the bigger life she'd always wanted, always dreamed of having. If she'd just said yes to his on-camera proposal.

But she hadn't. Regardless of how it had appeared, she hadn't. She'd said no.

Of course the general public didn't know that yet, only a select few insiders did. But still, she'd said no.

And she wasn't going to call and talk to Wes's secretary now, so she sent only a text message that yes, she had arrived safely in Northbridge. Then she added a cheery *Merry Christmas!*

Maybe just being near a jolly old Saint Nick was giving her some much-needed Christmas spirit.

Although when she returned her phone to the pocket of the knee-length navy blue wool coat she was wearing, and glanced at the skating teacher again, it struck her that this particular Saint Nick wasn't old at all. That behind the fake beard and mustache, under the red hat that he wore at a jaunty angle, was a much younger man with broad shoulders and impressively muscled legs that powered those skates expertly.

No, he was definitely not old. He was fit and trim and strong and…

And she didn't know what she was doing standing there ogling him. Especially when she knew she should be on her way.

Taking one more deep breath of the clear air and a last glance at the snow-covered town square, at the festively decorated octagonal-shaped gazebo at its center, and finally at the tiny skaters enthralled with the somehow-sexy-seeming Santa, Shannon got back into her sedan.

The fact that she would be seeing her new brother again made her want to make sure she didn't look too much the worse for wear from the drive, so she pulled down the visor above her and peered into the mirror on the underside of it.

She'd tied back her long, dark, walnut-colored hair into a ponytail in order to keep it neat. The plan had been a success because it looked the same as it had that morning. She wasn't sure she liked the new mascara she'd used to accentuate her blue-green eyes, but at least it had stayed on. So had the blush that dusted her cheekbones to add some pink to her pale skin and give her oval face some definition. But her glossy lipstick needed refreshing so she took the tube from her purse and did that.

Otherwise, she decided she was presentable enough to meet Chase Mackey where he lived with Hadley—the woman he was marrying on Saturday.

Take a left on South Street. Pass three mailboxes outside of town. Turn right at the fourth.

Shannon read her directions again to make sure she had the number of mailboxes correct.

She'd met Chase twice since he'd made contact with her, but he'd come to Billings each of those times—much the way her grandmother had over the years. This was Shannon's first trip to Northbridge since she was barely twelve.

According to Chase, he and his business partner Logan McKendrick had bought a section of an old farm that they had converted to meet their private and business needs. Logan lived in the original farmhouse. There was work space and a showroom for Mackey and McKendrick Furniture Designs as well as a loft where Chase lived, and a separate apartment he'd offered to Shannon for the holidays. So she wouldn't merely be visiting her newfound brother and the woman who would be his bride, she would apparently also be having a lot of contact with Logan and his family.

And with her nephew, Cody.

Cody was the fifteen-month-old son of Shannon and Chase's oldest sister. The death of Cody's mother was the reason Chase was now raising Cody, and what had revealed the far-reaching family ties that had brought Shannon and Chase together. Chase had brought the baby on both trips to Billings so Shannon had had the opportunity to meet the adorable baby and she couldn't wait to see him again.

She flipped the visor back up, and when she did she saw that the skating lesson had apparently ended because Santa and his not-quite-elves were all taking off their skates.

Thinking to leave before the parking lot got busy, Shannon buckled her seat belt and turned the key in the ignition.

Click, click, click. Nothing.

"How can that be, you just got me all the way to Northbridge?" she said to the thirteen-year-old car as she tried again.

But the same thing happened—a few clicks and nothing.

Not that time, not the next time, not the fourth time. The car just wouldn't start again.

And the only thing Shannon knew about a car was how to drive it.

"Great," she muttered.

As if something might have changed in the few minutes since she'd tried, she tried again, just as Santa was headed in her direction.

Still the engine wouldn't turn over. And then there Santa was, at the window right beside her, bent over so that a pair of thick-lashed, smoldering, coal-black eyes could peer in at her.

"Need help?"

He'd tied his black ice skates together by their laces and was wearing them slung over one shoulder as if having them there was second nature to him. The beard remained in place, but even from what she could see of his face she knew she'd been right in thinking that he wasn't *old* Saint Nick. The man appeared to be about her own age.

Shannon rolled down the window. "It won't start. There was no problem when I drove in. I stopped for two minutes and now it won't start again."

"Pop the hood and let me take a look," he suggested in a deep, deep voice.

Shannon had no idea if her roadside service could provide a rescue all the way in Northbridge, so this seemed like the next best thing. She pulled the lever that unlocked the hood and then got out of the car to join Santa in front of it.

He was tall. Of course he'd seemed tall compared to the kids who had surrounded him in the distance minutes earlier, but when Shannon stepped up beside him, she was surprised by just how tall he was—over six feet to her five-four. He was also much more massively muscled within that Santa suit than she'd realized.

And she had no idea why she was taking note of things like that…

He slipped his skates off his shoulder and set them on the ground. Then he found the latch that still held down the hood, released it and raised the heavy front cover of her car to expose the engine.

Shannon looked at it along with him even though she didn't have the foggiest idea what they were looking for.

"Your battery is new so it isn't that, and a jump won't get you going."

Oh, the wicked places her mind wandered to when he said that!

And again, she didn't know why. She didn't ordinarily have sex on the brain.

Silently scolding herself, she curbed her thoughts just as he said, "Let me try a couple of things. Get back in and turn it on when I holler for you to."

Shannon did as she was told but after several more attempts to get the engine to start whenever Santa told her to turn the key, it just didn't happen.

"I think you have something more going on than I can fix," he finally called to her.

Stepping out from behind the hood, he bent over, scooped up as much snow as he could and used it to clean his hands.

Shannon got out of the car and handed him several tissues she'd taken from her glove box.

"Well, thanks for trying," she said as he took the tissues to dry his hands. She nodded toward Main Street. "I saw a gas station up there—do you know if they have a mechanic?"

"Absolutely. The best—and only—one around here. I can give him a call for you, have him come down and take a look. He has a tow truck, too, if he needs to take it back to the station."

Shannon checked the time on her cell phone. The closing on her grandmother's property was in little more than an hour.

"I guess that would be good," she said tentatively. "Do you think the mechanic could come right down? I'm kind of in a hurry to get somewhere...."

"Even if he can't, you can just leave the keys under the seat and Roy—he's the mechanic—will take care of it. And if you need a lift somewhere, I can probably get you there."

Nice eyes or not, she wasn't getting into a car with a complete stranger.

"Thanks, but I can call my brother—"

"Who's your brother? It's a small town, I probably know him."

"Chase Mackey?"

"Shannon? Are you Shannon Duffy?" Santa asked.

"I am. How—"

"I'm Dag McKendrick—I'm the one you sold the farm to. Chase's partner, Logan, is my half brother."

The local Realtor had handled the sale. Shannon knew the name of her buyer, and that there was a family connection with her brother's partner, but they'd never met.

"Wow, this *is* a small town," she said, thinking about the coincidence.

"And I'm staying at Logan's place until I finish remodeling your grandmother's house. You're set to stay in the apartment above Logan's garage, right? So that must be where you're headed."

"Right."

"So we can call Roy and have him take a look at your car while you just go home with me."

Oh.

He made that sound as if everything had worked out perfectly. But Shannon still couldn't help being uncomfortable with the thought of taking everything this man said at face value and totally trusting him.

"Uhh…thanks, but—"

"Come on, it's fine. I even have candy…." he cajoled, taking a tiny candy cane from his pocket.

"You're a stranger masquerading as Santa Claus trying to lure me into a car with candy?" she said.

He laughed and while it wasn't a Santa-like *ho-ho-ho*, it was a great laugh.

"I guess that does sound bad, doesn't it?" he admitted. "Okay, how about this…"

He reached into one of the skates that he'd again slung over his shoulder and pulled out a wallet.

"Look—I'll prove who I am," he said, showing her his driver's license.

Shannon took a close look at it, particularly at the picture. For the kind of photograph that had a reputation for being notoriously bad, his was the exception. Not only were those eyes remarkable, but so was the rest of his face.

Roller-coaster-shaped lips. A slightly long, not-too-thin, not-too-thick nose that suited him. The shadow of a beard even though he was clean shaven, accentuating a sharp jawline and a squarish chin that dented upward in the center ever so alluringly.

And his hair—like the full eyebrows she could see for herself—was the color of espresso. It was so dark a brown it was just one shade shy of black, and he wore it short on the sides, a little long on top and disheveled to perfection.

And yes, the name on the license was, indeed, Daegal Pierson McKendrick.

"Daegal?" Shannon said as she read the unusual name.

"My mother had visions of glory. She thought it sounded European and sophisticated. My sisters are Isadora, Theodora and Zeli. But you can see that I am who I say I am. And in an hour and a half we'll be sitting across a table at the bank for the closing on your grandmother's property. Plus, tonight we're having a family dinner together, and we'll actually be living within spitting distance of each other even when we aren't together. I think you can risk a five-minute ride in my car."

Shannon had no idea why, but she couldn't resist giving him a hard time despite the abundance of reasons why she could trust him.

"How do I know that the person behind that beard is the person on this driver's license?"

He looked to his right, to his left, over his shoulder, making sure none of the children he'd been teaching to skate were around to see. Then he eased the beard down just enough for her to realize that in reality he was even better looking than in the photograph.

It was only a split-second glimpse, however, before he released the fluffy white disguise that must have been held on by elastic because it snapped back into place.

Then he waved a finger between the driver's license in her hand and himself and said, "Him, me, same guy. Not somebody who's gonna drive you out into the woods and ravage you."

Why did *that* make her smile? And maybe sound a little tantalizing?

She again had no answer to her own question but she did finally concede. "Okay. Let's call the mechanic and then I guess I'll *have* to trust you."

Dag McKendrick took a turn at smiling at her—a great smile that flashed flawlessly white teeth. "You don't *have* to trust me. You can walk—it's about four miles straight down South Street—five minutes by car, maybe an hour or more on foot, your choice…"

"I'll take the ride. But remember, the mechanic will know who I left with."

"And the possible future-Governor of Montana will

track me down and have me shot if anything happens to his soon-to-be wife."

So the news had even reached Northbridge. Shannon had been hoping that somehow the media coverage might have bypassed the small, secluded town during the two weeks since Wes's on-camera proposal.

But while she *wasn't* Wes Rumson's soon-to-be any-thing, she'd agreed not to refute it in public. She'd agreed to let Wes's press people handle it in a way that saved face for him, that didn't harm his bid for governor. And she couldn't blurt out the truth now, on the street, to someone she didn't know.

Even if she suddenly wanted to more than she had at any moment in the last two weeks.

Because, as she looked into Dag McKendrick's coal-black eyes, she hated the idea that he thought she was engaged when she wasn't.

And she didn't understand *that* any more than she'd understood any of the rest of her response to this man.

But that was what she'd agreed to and she had to stick to it.

She had to.

So she bit her tongue on the subject and merely said, "I'll get my suitcase out of the trunk while you call the mechanic. If you would, please."

"Already sounding gubernatorial," he teased.

Shannon merely rolled her eyes at him and reached beside the driver's seat to release the lever that opened the sedan's trunk.

"Just leave your suitcase, I'll get it," Dag McKendrick commanded as she headed for the rear of the car. "We can't have the future First Lady toting her own luggage."

Shannon ignored him and went for her suitcase anyway.

But as she was standing behind the car, she couldn't keep herself from peeking around the raised trunk cover at him, telling herself it was to make sure he was using the cell phone he'd taken from the inside of that same skate his wallet had been in, and not just to get another look at him.

Dag McKendrick.

Why on earth would she care if he thought she was engaged? she asked herself.

She still didn't have an answer.

But what she did have about five minutes later was a ride in a truck with Santa Claus behind the wheel, honking his horn and boisterously hollering *ho-ho-hos* to every child he drove by.

Chapter Two

On Thursday evening, in the upstairs guest room of his half brother's home, Dag set the packet of papers for the property he now owned in the top dresser drawer. As he did, the sounds of more and more voices began to rise up to him from the kitchen.

A family dinner to welcome Shannon Duffy and celebrate his new path in life as a land- and homeowner—that was what tonight was, what was beginning to happen downstairs.

It was a nice sound and he sat on the edge of the bed to give himself a minute to just listen to it from a distance.

And to stretch his knee and rub some of the ache out of it.

He should have used the elastic support brace on the ice today but he hadn't thought that teaching preschoolers to skate would put as much strain on his knee as it had. Plus he knew he was sloughing off when it came to things like that because on the whole, the knee was fine and didn't need any bracing. It had been that quick rush to the kid who had fallen—that's when he'd jimmied things up a little.

But just a little. The pain lotion he'd rubbed into it after his shower this afternoon had helped, the massage was helping, too, and he thought it would be fine by tomorrow. Every now and then it just liked to let him know that the doctors, the trainers, the coaches, the physical therapists had all been right—there was no way he could have gone on to play hockey again.

And he wasn't going to. After returning to Northbridge in late September he'd done some house-hunting, and he was now the owner of his own forty-seven acres of farm and ranch land, of a house that was going to be really nice once he was finished remodeling and updating it. He was on that new path that was being celebrated tonight and he'd be damned if he was going to do any more mourning of what wasn't to be.

He'd had a decent run in professional hockey. Hockey and the endorsements that went with a successful career had set him up financially. And even if it hadn't been his choice to move on, even if moving on had happened a lot earlier than he'd hoped it would, a lot earlier than he'd expected it would, he was still glad to be back in Northbridge.

The positives were the things he was going to concentrate on—the new path, getting back to his hometown and the fact that it was Christmastime. The fact that this was the first Christmas in years that he was home well in advance of the holiday, with family. The fact that he didn't have to rush in after a Christmas Eve game or rush out for a December twenty-sixth game. The fact that he wasn't in a hospital or a physical therapy rehab center the way he had been the last two Christmases.

So things might not be exactly the way he'd planned, but they were still good. And he still considered himself a pretty lucky guy. A little older, a little wiser, but still pretty lucky. Lucky enough to have been able to go on.

The sound of a woman's laughter drifted up to him then and he listened more intently.

Had Shannon Duffy come across the backyard from the garage apartment?

And why should he care whether she had or not?

He shouldn't.

He didn't.

But when he heard the laugh again and recognized it as his half sister Hadley's laugh, he stayed put, continuing to rub his knee rather than go down the way he might have otherwise.

It was just good manners, he told himself. They were sort of the co-guests-of-honor. If Shannon was here, he should go down. If she wasn't here yet, there was no rush.

Yeah, right, it's just manners…

Okay, maybe he didn't hate the idea that he was going to get to see her again. But only because she made for a pleasant view.

Dark, thick, silky, walnut-colored hair around that pale peaches-and-cream skin. A thin, straight nose that came to a slight point on the end that turned up just a touch. Lips that were soft and shiny and too damn kissable to bear. Rosy cheeks that made her look healthy and glowing from the inside out. Eyes that at first had seemed blue—a pale, luminous blue—and then had somehow taken on a green hue, too, to blend them into the color of sea and sky together. And a compact little body that was just tight enough, just round enough, just right…

A beauty—that's what Shannon Duffy was. No doubt about it. So much of a beauty that he hadn't been able to get the image of her out of his head even after he'd left her to her brother this afternoon when he'd come up here to shower.

So much of a beauty that he'd had to rein in the urge to stare at her every time he'd had the opportunity to see her today.

No wonder she'd snagged herself a Rumson….

Wes Rumson, the newest Golden Boy of the Montana clan that had forever been the biggest name in politics in the state. It had been all over the news a couple weeks ago that not only was he going to run for governor, he was also engaged to Shannon Duffy. When Dag had heard that, he'd figured that was the reason she was selling her grandmother's property.

It was also one of the reasons that no matter how great-looking she was, he would be keeping his distance from her.

Engaged, dating, separated—even flirting with someone else—any woman with the faintest hint of involvement or connection or ties to another guy and there was no way Dag would get anywhere near her. And not only because he wasn't a woman-poacher—which he wasn't.

He'd learned painfully and at the wrong end of a crowbar that if a woman wasn't completely and totally free and available, having anything whatsoever to do with her could be disastrous.

So, beautiful, not beautiful, he wouldn't go anywhere near Shannon Duffy.

At least not anywhere nearer than anyone else who

was about to share the holiday with her as part of a larger group.

Nope, Shannon Duffy was absolutely the same as the decorations on the Christmas tree, as the lights and holly and pine boughs and ribbons all over this house, all over town—she was something pretty to look at and nothing more.

But damn, no one could say she wasn't pretty to look at.…

"A neckruss goes on your neck, a brace-a-let goes on your wristle."

"Right," Shannon confirmed with a smile at three-year-old Tia McKendrick's pronunciation of things.

After a lovely dinner of game hen, wild rice, roasted vegetables and salad, followed by a dessert of fruit cobbler and ice cream, everyone was still sitting around the table in the dining room of Logan and Meg McKendrick's home.

Wine had also been in abundance and had left Shannon more relaxed than when she'd arrived this evening. She assumed the same was true for her dinner companions because no one seemed in any hurry to get up and clear the remainder of the dishes.

Tia, on the other hand, had ventured from her seat to sit on Shannon's lap and explore the simple circle bracelet and plain gold chain necklace that Shannon had worn with her sweater set and slacks tonight.

"Can I see the brace-a-let?" Tia requested.

"You can," Shannon granted, taking it off and handing it to the small curly-haired girl.

Looking on from Shannon's right were Meg and Logan—Tia's stepmother and father.

To Shannon's left were Chase and his soon-to-be bride, Hadley—who also happened to be Logan's sister.

On Hadley's lap was fifteen-month-old Cody, and directly across from Shannon was Dag.

Which made it difficult for her not to look at him in all his glory dressed in jeans and a fisherman's knit sweater, his well-defined jaw clean shaven and yet still slightly shadowed with the heaviness of his beard.

Their positioning at the table apparently made it difficult for him not to look at her, too, because his dark eyes seemed to have been on her most of the night.

"I think that brace-a-let is kind of big for you, Miss Tia," Dag said then. "You can get both of your wristles in it."

Tia tried that, putting her tiny hands through the hoop from opposite directions as if it were a muff. Then, giggling and holding up her arms for everyone to see, she said, "Look it, I can!"

That caught Cody's interest and the infant leaned far forward to try to take the bracelet for himself. Luckily Shannon had worn two, so she took off the other one and handed it to the baby. Who promptly put it in his mouth.

"So, Shannon, you're pretty much a stranger to Northbridge even though your grandmother lived here?" Logan asked then.

"I am. I only visited here a few times growing up and that was all before I was twelve. Between my parents' business and their health, there was just no getting away."

"What was their business?" Hadley asked.

"They owned a small shoe repair and leather shop, and the building it was in. We lived above the shop and they couldn't afford help—they worked the shop themselves six days a week—so in order to leave town, they had to close down and that was too costly for them. Gramma would come to visit us—even for holidays. Plus with my parents' health problems they were both sort of doing the best they could just to get downstairs, put in a day's work and go back up to the apartment."

"Did they have serious health problems long before they died?" Chase asked.

"My mom and dad's health problems were definitely serious and started *long* before they died," Shannon confirmed. "As a young man, my dad was in an accident that cost him one kidney and damaged his other—the damaged one continued to deteriorate from the injury, though, and he eventually had to go on dialysis. My mom had had rheumatic fever as a kid and it took a toll on her heart, which also made her lungs weak and caused her to be just generally unwell."

"I'm a little surprised that people in that kind of physical shape were allowed to adopt a child," Meg observed.

"The situation at the time helped that," Shannon said. "What I was told was that my birth parents were killed in a car accident—"

"True," Chase confirmed.

"There wasn't anything about other kids in the story," Shannon continued. "I didn't know there was an older sister who had a different father to take her, or that there was an older brother and twin younger brothers, that's for sure. What my parents said was just that there wasn't any family to take me, that the reverend here had put out feelers for someone else to. When my parents asked if that could be them, the reverend helped persuade the authorities to let them have me despite their health issues—which weren't as bad at the time, anyway."

"I don't know if you know or not, but that reverend is my grandfather," Meg said.

"Really? No, I didn't know that."

"And sick or not, your folks must have wanted a child a lot," Hadley concluded.

"A lot," Shannon confirmed. "But having one of their own just wasn't possible."

"Did you have a good life with them?" Chase asked.

Despite the two occasions when she and Chase had met in Billings and the few phone calls and emails they'd exchanged, they'd barely scratched the surface of getting to know each other. And while she was aware that Chase's upbringing in foster care had been somewhat dour, Shannon hadn't gotten into what her own growing-up years had been like.

"I didn't have a lot of material things," she told him now. "But no one was more loved than I was. My parents were wonderful people who adored each other and who thought I was just a gift from heaven," she said with a small laugh to hide the tears that the memory brought to her eyes. She also glanced downward at Tia still playing with the bracelet in her lap and smoothed the little girl's hair.

When the tears were under control and she glanced up again, she once more found Dag watching her, this time with a warmth that inexplicably wrapped around her and comforted her before she told herself that she had to be imagining it.

"It must have been so hard for you to lose them," Meg said, interrupting that split-second moment.

"It was," Shannon answered, forcing herself to look away from Dag. "But at the same time, they had both gotten so sick. That's why my grandmother left Northbridge a few years ago—to help me take care of them when it was just more than I could do on my own—"

"You took care of them?" Dag asked in a voice that sounded almost as if it was for her ears only.

"I did—happily, and they made it as easy as they could, but I still had to work, too, and do what I could to help the man I'd hired to keep the business running. Plus my parents needed someone with them during the day, as well, so Gramma came to stay. By the time my dad died last January I couldn't wish him another day of suffering just so I could go on having him with me. And he and my mom were so close that she just couldn't go on without him. I think her heart really did break then, so it was no shock when she died just months later. And to tell you the truth, after spending every day of their adult lives together—working together, going up to the apartment together, never being without each other—it sort of seemed as if they belonged together in whatever afterlife there might be, too."

"And then there was just you and your grandmother?" Dag asked, his eyes still on her in that penetrating gaze.

"Right, Gramma was still with me. And she seemed healthy as ever. She helped me go through all my parents' things—personal and financial and business. She helped me find an apartment so we could sell the business and the building it was in. She helped me move. She was just about to come back to Northbridge—which was what she really wanted to do for herself—when she had a heart attack in August. She didn't make it through that...."

This time Shannon shrugged her shoulders to draw attention away from the moisture gathering in her eyes. When she could, she said, "Strange as it may sound, my grandmother's death was actually the shock."

"And just like that—within a matter of eight months—you lost your whole family?" Hadley marveled sadly. "Chase said you had taken some time off from teaching kindergarten then, and it's no wonder!"

"But now she has Chase and two more brothers out there somewhere who she and Chase are going to find," Meg reminded, obviously attempting to inject something lighter into the conversation.

Shannon looked at her newly discovered brother. "Whatever I can do on that score…" she said to him.

"I've hit a wall trying to find the twins," Chase said. "I'm thinking about hiring a private investigator after the first of the year. But we can talk about that later."

To change the subject completely then, Shannon said, "So I know Chase and Logan grew up together as best friends and then traveled the country and ended up starting Mackey and McKendrick Furniture Designs, but were you all friends in school?"

"Actually, no," Meg answered. "I know—small town, you'd think we would have lived in each other's back pockets. But I was younger than Chase and Logan, so I was barely aware of who they were and they say the same thing about me. I knew Hadley a little better, but again, we weren't the same age, so we didn't hang out together."

"But, Hadley, if Logan and Chase were close, you must have known Chase," Shannon observed.

"Oh, she knew him all right," Dag said, goading his half sister.

Hadley didn't rise to the bait beyond throwing her cloth napkin at him before she said, "I knew Chase. I had the biggest crush on him *ever*. But we didn't get together until this past September when he moved back here—"

"When I really got to know her," Chase contributed, putting his arm around the back of Hadley's chair and leaning in to kiss her.

And why, when Shannon averted her eyes, her gaze landed instead on Dag, she didn't know. But there they were, suddenly sharing a glance while the soon-to-be-married couple shared a kiss. And to Shannon it almost seemed as if something couple-ish passed between them, too.

Which, of course, couldn't possibly have been the case and she again questioned what was going on with her.

Wanting whatever it was interrupted, she focused on Logan to say, "And there are three more McKendrick sisters with unusual names, right?"

"And another McKendrick brother—Tucker," Logan answered. "You'll meet them all tomorrow night at the rehearsal and dinner."

Cody threw Shannon's bracelet then, letting everyone know that he was no longer content.

"Oh-oh, I think it's past a couple of bedtimes," Meg said.

"Not me!" Tia insisted. She was still on Shannon's lap but now she'd taken off her shoes and was trying unsuccessfully to put both of her feet through Shannon's bracelet.

"Yes, you, too," Logan interjected.

"And that's our cue for dish duty," Chase added with a grimace tossed at his friend.

"That was the deal," Hadley reminded. "Meg and I will put kids to bed, Logan and Chase get to show what they learned as dishwashers on their grand tour of the country, and Dag and Shannon are off the hook because the dinner was for them."

"I don't mind helping with clean-up," Shannon said.

"Shhh," Dag put in. "Don't ruin a good thing."

"Besides," Meg added. "You've had a long day, Shannon. You drove the whole way in from Billings and had the closing, and all of us plying you with questions tonight. You have to be worn out. I know I would be."

"How about if I walk you out to the apartment?" Dag offered before she could respond to what Meg had said.

"Oh. You don't have to do that," Shannon demurred, not because she didn't want him to, but because the minute he suggested it she wanted him to *too* much....

"I think that's a great idea—Dag *should* walk Shannon to the apartment so she doesn't just have to trudge out there alone," Meg agreed.

"Really—"

"Go on," Hadley urged. "I'd walk with you but I have to get all of Cody's gear ready to take with me to our place."

The spacious, luxurious loft was what Hadley was referring to. It was in the building beside the apartment over the garage where Shannon was staying. The same building that housed the work space and showroom for Mackey and McKendrick Furniture Designs on the ground floor.

Hadley's urging seemed to have ended the discussion because everyone got up from the table and Meg came to take Tia from Shannon's lap.

"Give back Shannon's bracelet and tell her thank you for letting you play with it," Meg told the three-year-old.

"I could keep it...." Tia whispered to Shannon.

"No, you can't keep it," Meg said before Shannon had the chance to answer, taking the bracelet from Tia and the other one from where Cody had thrown it, and giving them both to Shannon just before she picked up Tia.

Shannon said her good-nights while Dag ran upstairs for a jacket. A brown leather motorcycle jacket that made him look every inch a bad boy when he returned with it on.

But Shannon told herself that wasn't anything she should be noticing. Or appreciating. And she curbed it.

She had her own coat on by that time, too, and the next thing she knew, they were out the back door and into the cold, crisp night.

"It's so quiet here," she said softly when Dag had closed the door behind them.

"A nice change from inside?"

"It wasn't that dinner wasn't nice," she was quick to say as they headed for the garage in the distance, not wanting him to think there was anything about the evening that she hadn't enjoyed. "I guess it's just that I'm not used to having so much family around."

"Because there was always just your mother, father and grandmother?" Dag said as they fell easily into step with each other.

"Yes. And really, until the last few years, it was just my parents and me. But here I am now with a brother and a nephew and Hadley will be my sister-in-law, and there's all of you McKendricks, too, who seem to be like family to Chase—"

"Not to mention two more brothers if and when you find them," Dag reminded.

"It's a lot for someone who's always been part of a small group, a small life."

"A small life?" Dag repeated with a laugh. "What exactly does that mean?"

"You know, just a small, simple, workaday life. Certainly no living in Italy and France the way Hadley did. Or even the kind of travel Chase and Logan did around the country for years. Teaching kindergarten isn't a high-powered career. I've been to a few fancy parties with Wes, and there was a trip to Europe, but I haven't done anything that would qualify as a *big* life."

"So far," Dag amended. "But marrying into a rich and powerful family and possibly becoming the First Lady of Montana? That ought to pump up the volume considerably."

Shannon hoped that dropping her head when he said that only seemed to be because she was watching her first step up the outer wooden staircase alongside the garage to the apartment. But really she was hiding her expression so she didn't give away that she wasn't going to *pump up the volume* of her life by marrying Wes Rumson.

"Becoming the First Lady of Montana would be a bigger life all right," she muttered noncommittally. "And a bigger life is always what I've wanted. But we were talking about what I'm used to and neither a bigger life nor a lot of large family gatherings like tonight are it."

"So you'll have some adjusting to do and tonight was good practice," Dag said as he followed her up the stairs.

"Tonight was just nice," she said quietly again.

They reached the landing and she unlocked the apartment door, reaching inside to turn on the light and wondering suddenly if she should invite Dag in. She couldn't think of any reason why she should. And yet she felt some inclination to do it anyway.

"Want to hide out here until the dishes are done?" she asked with a nod in the direction of the main house where Chase and Logan were visible through the window over the sink.

Dag glanced in that direction, too, but then brought his gaze back to her, accompanied by a grin that was disarmingly handsome. And made her think that he was tempted to accept her invitation to stay.

But after a moment he seemed to fight the urge and said, "I might not have been able to hold my own with those two when I was eight and they were making me pick up their smelly socks, but now? They don't get anything over on me."

Still, he didn't seem in any hurry to go and Shannon wasn't sure what to do about that. Standing there facing him, staring up into features any movie star could have used to advantage, wasn't giving her answers.

Then Dag said, "Those movers you hired to pack everything and clear out your grandmother's house missed a few things. Nothing big—just some odds and ends I've come across working on the place—"

"Like?"

"Like some clothes and a blanket that were stuffed up high in a closet. Some kitchen things. A couple pictures that had fallen behind a drawer. An old jewelry box—I can't even remember what all. I've been putting them in boxes when I come across them because I didn't know if there was anything you might want—"

"Most of what the movers brought to Billings I sold in a yard sale at a friend's house. There was so much of it that I can't imagine that they missed anything."

"Like I said, I don't think there's anything important. It's stuff that was probably jammed somewhere because not even your grandmother needed or wanted it. But still,

I don't want to be the one to throw out anything that isn't mine. There's only two boxes and I can bring them home, but I thought you might want to see what I'm doing to the place. Maybe have one more walk through it for old time's sake..."

Was that what was appealing to her about his suggestion?

Or was it the thought of going out to the ranch and seeing him?

It had to be the nostalgia—the house *had* been her grandmother's after all. And she had spent some time there with her grandmother when she was a child.

Plus there *was* some curiosity to see what Dag was doing to the place, she told herself. That had to be what was behind her wanting to take him up on his offer.

"I think I might like to walk through the place one more time," she said. "Just tell me when it's convenient for you."

His grin returned even bigger than it had been before, but Shannon refused to allow herself to read anything into it—like the fact that maybe he wanted the visit from her just to see her, too....

"Tomorrow? I'll be working out there all day. You can swing by anytime."

"Shall I take your cell phone number and call first?"

"Nah. Anytime. Sleep in in the morning, unpack, do whatever you had planned and when it works out for you, just drive over."

"Okay."

And why did they go on standing there, looking at each other as if there should be more to say?

Shannon didn't know but that's what they were doing—

she was just looking up into those black, black eyes of his, lost a little in them....

Then he finally broke their stare. "Great. I'll see you tomorrow, then."

"Sometime tomorrow," she reiterated, thinking that the minute it came out of her mouth it sounded stupid.

But it didn't seem to affect Dag because he just tossed her another thousand-watt smile and turned on his heels on the landing. Then he called a good-night over one of those broad shoulders and went back down the steps.

Which was when Shannon stepped into the warmth of the apartment and closed the door.

And realized that she was suddenly eager to get to bed, to get to sleep, to get tomorrow to come.

Chapter Three

"Yes, I got here, I did the closing on Gramma's farm yesterday, and it's nice to be spending time with Chase and Cody—I had breakfast and lunch with them and Hadley, and then Hadley took me to have my bridesmaid's dress fitted so it will be ready for the wedding tomorrow. And tonight is the rehearsal and the rehearsal dinner," Shannon said into the phone.

"Doesn't sound like you're missing me at all," Wes Rumson said on the other end.

"Wes..."

"I know, there's no reason you should be missing me—even if we *were* engaged you were used to not having me around for most things. It's the curse of the Rumson men."

And of his own parents' marriage and one of the reasons Shannon had turned down his proposal.

But she didn't say that.

Instead she said, "I appreciate that you called, though." Which was true. She honestly did hope they could remain friends.

"It feels a little weird to be so included in this wedding," she admitted then. "Hadley told me it was important to her and to Chase that the family he's found be a part of everything. But as nice as they all are—and they all are wonderfully nice people—they're still basically strangers to me."

Wes made no comment and she had the sense that he was at least half occupied with something other than their conversation.

Still, she felt the need to fill the silence he'd left and she said, "How are things going on your end?"

"Great!" Wes said in his most enthusiastic politician's voice. "We're looking good in the polls, we'll likely have the endorsements we need, even the President has promised to stop here sometime in the spring to throw his weight behind me."

"So maybe this would be a good time to make the announcement that there isn't any engagement...."

"I keep hoping we might not have to make that announcement."

"Wes—"

"The voters love you, Shannon. They love the idea of a little romance in the wings, of a wedding. And you know how I feel...."

That what the voters loved was of first and foremost importance to him? That how he felt about her was merely an afterthought?

But Shannon didn't say what ran through her mind. Instead she said, "You have to make the announcement, Wes."

"The First Lady of Montana—that would be the

Bigger Life you've always wanted," he said as if he were dangling a carrot in front of a donkey's nose. *Bigger Life* was the way he'd come to refer to her desire—as if it were an entity of its own. "No tiny apartment above a shoe repair shop—you'd live in the Governor's mansion. And this is only the start—you know we're shooting for the White House. You can't get a *Bigger Life* than that."

"I couldn't marry you just to have a bigger life, Wes. Any more than you should marry me to win votes."

"That's not fair—we talked about getting married before—"

And even then Shannon had had doubts about it. Yes, she'd always wanted a life that was bigger than the very small, limited life her parents had lived and Wes knew that. But when it came to a relationship, to marriage, she wanted exactly what her parents had had. And that wasn't the way she felt about Wes. She knew that wasn't the way Wes felt about her. Which was the *real* reason she'd said no.

"You don't really want to go over this again, do you?" she cajoled.

This time rather than silence giving away the fact that Wes's attention was split, he proved it by saying something away from the phone to someone else.

And since he never did answer her question, Shannon let it drop so she could persist with what she needed to get through to him. "I'm sorry, Wes, but you need to break the news publicly. And isn't sooner better than later? Don't you want to get it out there and get it over with so it will be genuinely old news and forgotten by election day?"

"Rumsons aren't quitters, Shannon. If there's any chance—"

"But there isn't," she said as kindly as she could. "I'm not an undecided voter who needs to be swayed, Wes. This really is just a no."

"Because of that Beverly Hills deal," he accused. "When it comes to a Bigger Life, Shannon, wiping the noses of movie stars' and moguls' kids can't compare to being—"

The hanger-on to Wes's Bigger Life?

Shannon thought that but she didn't say it. What she said was, "The *Beverly Hills deal* was also not the reason I said no—I told you that, too. It's just a new avenue I may take. But no matter what, Wes, you need to have your public relations group get on the announcement that there isn't any engagement. Even people in the boonies of Northbridge think I'm going to marry you."

"Then let's not disappoint them."

Shannon closed her eyes, dropped her face forward and shook her head. "Wes…"

"All right, I have to hang up, too," he said as if their exchange had involved something different than it had. "I'll check with you in a couple of days to make sure you're still okay. But if you need anything—anything at all, day or night—"

"I know I can call you. I appreciate that." Even though she also knew that rather than reach him, her call would automatically be rerouted to his voice mail or his secretary or his campaign manager—depending on how many numbers she tried—and that there would never be an immediate callback. Like when her grandmother had died so suddenly…

They said their goodbyes and Shannon hung up.

With a quick glance at the time, she grabbed her car keys and went out the apartment's door and down the steps to her car—freshly back from the local garage where it had required a new starter.

Wes's call was making her late. Dag had said she could come by her grandmother's house anytime to see what he was doing with the place and to pick up what remained of her grandmother's things, but it was already after four and she was afraid he would give up on her. And she didn't want that.

Behind the wheel, she turned the key in the ignition and was pleased to see that the repair had been a good one—the engine started on the first try.

On her way to what was formerly her grandmother's place, she kept an eye out for Dag's big electric-blue truck coming in the opposite direction, just in case, and that was all it took to replace thoughts of Wes with thoughts of Dag.

Until she turned onto the road that led to her grandmother's house and it came into view.

The two-story wedding cake–shaped farmhouse was the home her grandmother had come to as a bride. Shannon's eyes filled with tears when she suddenly pictured her grandmother sitting on the big front porch, snapping green beans fresh from the garden.

She missed her so much.…

She missed them all so much.…

But even though the memories of being at that house brought on some pain as Shannon parked in front of it, she wasn't sorry she'd come. To her this was still her grandmother's house no matter who owned it on paper and she did want to touch base with it one last time.

Then the front door opened and Dag McKendrick appeared behind the screen. And somehow seeing him bolstered her and made it easier for her to actually go through with it.

As she turned off the engine, Dag shouldered his way out onto the porch. He was wearing jeans that Wes wouldn't have considered owning—low-slung and faded. Wes also would have had no use for the equally antique chambray shirt that Dag wore over a white T-shirt peeking above the unfastened top two buttons.

Shannon wasn't sure why she was mentally comparing the two men but she couldn't seem to stop herself as she took in the sight of Dag's shirtsleeves rolled midway up his massive forearms. Drying his hands on a small towel, he tossed her a smile that wasn't at all the kind of practiced-in-case-a-photographer-might-be-nearby smile she knew she would have received from Wes.

Both men were handsome, she admitted, but in different ways. There was never a hair out of place on Wes's dusty blond head while disarray was part of the style for Dag's dark locks. Wes was lean and wiry and stiff backed where Dag was muscular and powerful looking, his posture relaxed—as if his confidence came from knowing he could handle himself rather than from the entitlement that came with being a Rumson.

Rugged versus refined—that's what Shannon concluded. Dag's good looks were rough and earthy, while Wes's were polished and sophisticated.

"Hey there! I was beginning to give up on you," Dag called to her as he came down off the porch.

And that was when it struck Shannon that it wasn't only their looks that were different.

Wes would have waited for her within the shelter of the house. He wouldn't have come out into the cold December afternoon to greet her. But that was what Dag did. Because their styles were entirely different. While Wes was known for his charisma, what she'd already seen from Dag just in the brief time since they'd met was a special brand of charm that—while equally as smooth—was more natural than slick.

And when it came to sex appeal?

When it came to sex appeal, Shannon had no idea why anything like *that* had even popped into her mind as Dag opened her door.

She recalled belatedly that he'd said something a split second earlier that she'd heard through her closed window.

What was it…?

Ah, that he'd just about given up on her.…

"I'm sorry I'm so late. It took longer with the seamstress than I expected it to and then I had a phone call I had to take. I kept an eye out for your truck the whole way here in case I passed you on the road."

"Another ten minutes or so and you would have."

And the sound of his voice—there was absolutely no reason why she liked the deeper timbres of Dag Mc-Kendrick's voice better than the slightly higher octave of Wes's but in that instant it struck her that she did.

Then she told herself to stop this right now! She had no interest in this man. He was nothing but a friend of her brother's and the buyer of her grandmother's house and someone she just happened to be acquainted with for the time being. Her relationship with Wes was barely cold—not even cold enough for anyone else to know about. Her entire life had changed in the last year, she could very well be headed to a new life in Beverly Hills, and in all of that there was no room, no time, no reason, for her to be even remotely interested in this man.

And she wasn't.

She wasn't…

"Is it too late? Do you need to get home?" she asked then, stiffening her spine a bit to resist his appeal.

"Nah. We can have a little time here and still get back for a shower before the rehearsal."

Had he meant to say that as if they'd be showering together? Or was this just another of those crazy blips that made her mind wander into territory where it had no business going?

"Not that *we'll* be showering. What I meant was that *I'll* still be able to get back to take a shower," he amended then, letting her know that she hadn't misheard him. But the cocky grin that went with the amendment told her that the slip of tongue didn't embarrass him at all.

Mischief and teasing—two more things Wes never indulged in. Not even with her, let alone with someone he barely knew.

"Yeah, I think I'll leave you alone to shower," Shannon answered the way she would have addressed a kindergartner who had said something inappropriate, even if she couldn't help smiling at their exchange.

"Probably for the best," he said, undaunted by her tone.

"I didn't realize the outside of the house needed painting so badly," Shannon said as she got out of the car, staring at the farmhouse in order to avoid looking at Dag and obviously changing the subject.

"Yep. I don't know when your grandmother had it done last but it has to have been decades ago. It'll all have to be scraped and power-washed then re-primed. What do you think about the color when I get around to painting? Back to the yellow or shall I go with white?"

"I know I don't really get a vote, but I always liked it yellow—it looked warm and homey and sunny to me that way."

"Trimmed in white?"

"I would, but it's your house now."

Dag motioned for her to go ahead of him up the porch steps and when they reached the house, he held the screen door open for her.

There were no signs of her grandmother in what Shannon stepped into. The inside of the house was empty of furniture and all the rooms she could see from the entry were in various stages of repair, remodel or renovation with the necessary tools and supplies littering them.

"Wow, you're really gutting the place," Shannon observed. "I know the appraiser said it needed work—that was why I reduced the price—but I had no idea it was this extensive."

"How long has it been since you were here?"

"The summer just before I turned twelve, so almost eighteen years...."

"Things were pretty run-down."

"My grandfather died the year before I was here last, I guess Gramma must not have kept up with things as well on her own. I didn't realize."

"From what you said about your folks last night, it sounded like you had enough to deal with."

"And it wasn't as if my dad could come here and help her out, or send money for her to hire someone," Shannon added as they pieced together why her grandmother must have let the place fall into such disrepair. "But I'm sorry if you came in on a big mess—I had no idea...."

"It was just an old house. I would have wanted to update it anyway. No big deal. And there are some pluses to the place—the crown molding everywhere, the hardwood floors and just the way the whole house is built makes it more sound and sturdy than newer construction. It gives me a good foundation to work from. Come on, I'll walk you through what I have planned."

They spent the next half hour going room to room,

with Dag explaining a complete plumbing overhaul that would leave all three bathrooms like new, a kitchen that sounded like it would be a chef's dream come true, and even ideas for accent colors of paint here and there that left Shannon surprised by his good taste.

When they reached the upstairs bedroom where she'd stayed on her visits here, Shannon said, "Have you found the secret cubby?"

Dag's eyebrows shot up in curiosity. "There's a secret cubby? Whatever that is…"

"I'll show you."

Shannon knelt down in front of a section of flowered wallpaper a few feet to the right of the closet. It didn't look any different than the rest of the loud pink tea-rose print but when she pressed inward and then did a quick release, that particular section popped open to reveal a two-foot-by-two-foot hole in the wall.

Dag laughed. "I'm sure I would have found that when I stripped off the wallpaper, but I had no idea it was there."

"It makes a great hiding place," Shannon said, peering inside to see if the things she'd hidden in it long, long ago could still be there.

They were.

"Let's see," she said as she began pulling them out.

Dag hunkered down on his haunches beside her to have a closer look.

"This is the notebook I brought with me on my last trip—I was going to write a novel in it. An entire novel that I would write in secret and then surprise everyone with when I was finished."

"At eleven?"

"Uh-huh. I believe I wrote about two paragraphs…" she said as she turned the notebook upright and unveiled the first page. "Yep, two paragraphs. That was as far as my career as a great American novelist went. And I think it's for the best," she added with a laugh after glancing at what she'd written.

Then she set the notebook down and reached back into the cubby.

"Let me guess—those were from your great American artist period?" Dag teased when she pulled out several pages cut from a coloring book.

Shannon flipped through the sheets. "Not a single stroke outside the lines—I was proud of being so meticulous. I think I was six."

"And this? You were going to be a chess master?" Dag said, picking up a carved horse's head chess piece that had come out with the coloring book pages.

Shannon grimaced. "*That* was me being a brat."

"You were a brat?" he said as if the idea delighted him.

"I was five," she said. "You have to understand, my parents were so close, so devoted to each other, so happy just to be together, that sometimes I felt a little left out. Not that I actually was," she defended them in a hurry. "I was actually about as spoiled as I could be with their limited resources. But at five, when they were talking and laughing over a chess game..." Shannon shrugged. "One of those times I tried to interfere by—"

"Stealing one of their chessmen so they couldn't play?"

"And hiding it," Shannon confessed. "I was leaving to come here the next day and I stuck it in my suitcase, so I ended up bringing it with me. By the time I was supposed to go home, I didn't want to bring it back and admit I'd taken it and get into trouble, so I put it in the cubby."

"Shame on you," Dag pretended to reprimand, but it came with a laugh.

"I know. Of course as I got older, the kind of relationship my parents had was what I realized I wanted for myself, but as a very little kid, there were times when I resented it because they were just so content being together no matter what they were doing—watching their favorite TV show or movie, or doing puzzles, or just talking or—"

"Playing chess?"

"Or playing chess. *I* wanted to be the center of their universe—and I was—but they were also the center of each other's universe, if that makes any sense..." Another shrug. "I think maybe I was a little jealous—it wasn't rational, I was a kid."

"And now have you found that kind of relationship for yourself with the potential future-Governor?"

There was no way she could answer that and luckily at about that same moment, she spotted one more thing in the cubby and reached in to retrieve a very ragged stuffed dog.

"Oh, Poppy! I'd forgotten all about you," she said as if she hadn't heard Dag's question.

She didn't know if he recognized that she didn't want to answer him or just went with the flow, but he didn't push it. Instead he said, "That is one ratty-looking toy."

"I know. I carried him around with me, slept with him, played with him—he was my constant companion. When I got too old for that I couldn't stand the thought that he might get thrown away, so I brought him here with me and put him in the cubby for safekeeping."

She checked out the old toy, saying as she did, "Poor Poppy, I never sucked my thumb, but I chewed off both of his ears, he lost an eye and his nose, and my mom had to sew the holes. His tail is gone, and his seams split and had to be fixed more times than I can remember—he's kind of a mess."

"He looks well loved," Dag decreed, and Shannon appreciated that that was the perspective he took when she knew that Wes would have been impatient with her sentimentality over it.

But Dag even waited while she hugged it for a moment before she set it down and took the last few items out of the cubby.

"Love notes," she confided as if they were a deep, dark secret. "This was from the summer I was ten—I was at camp just before I came to see Gramma and I had a sizzling romance with one of the boys there...."

"How sizzling could it have been at ten?"

"Hot, hot, hot!" Shannon said with a laugh. "He sat next to me on movie night and held my hand when the lights went out. And look at these notes—he thought I had nice teeth. And my woven pot holder was the best in the whole class. And he liked my eyes because they match! How much more sizzling do you want it?"

"Oh, yeah, it doesn't get better than that!" Dag agreed facetiously. "This cubby-thing is a treasure trove."

"Ah, but it looks like that's it," Shannon complained after poking her head into the cubby to make sure. "Now the place is all yours."

Which struck her with a sudden, unexpected sadness that made her think that maybe she had a few more attachments to her grandmother's house than she'd originally thought.

But it was done and she knew from the way Dag had talked about his plans for the remodel that he loved the place, so she comforted herself with that—and by petting her old stuffed dog the way she had when she'd needed solace as a kid.

"I'll get a box for this stuff," Dag suggested then, as if he knew she could use a minute alone with her things, with the cubby, with the house. She was grateful for that, and once he'd gotten to his feet and left the room, she swiveled around to take one last glance at it.

The wallpaper was gaudy and overwhelming but she still had fond memories of being here with her grandmother on those few visits, of the fact that despite not spending much time here, it had still felt like an extension of home.

"I think he'll take good care of your house, though, Gramma," she whispered as if her grandmother might be listening.

Then Dag came back with a cardboard box.

"It must be late—it's starting to get dark," Shannon said with a glance out the window as she accepted the box from Dag. "We should probably be going."

"Probably," Dag confirmed, holding out a hand to help her to her feet once everything was in the box.

She could have stood without aid but she didn't want to offend him by refusing, so she accepted the hand up.

"Thanks," she said, wishing she wasn't quite so aware of how big and strong and warm his hand was. And how well hers fit into it.

But wishing didn't make that awareness go away and as soon as she could, she took her hand back. Somehow regretting it when she had—another of those crazy blips, she decided.

Dag seemed completely oblivious to the odd effects he could have on her and once she was on her own again, he bent over and picked up the box. He tucked it neatly under one arm and motioned for her to lead the way out.

"I have a favor to ask you," Shannon said as they went back downstairs.

"Sure," Dag responded without hesitation as he set the box from upstairs on top of the two boxes of things he'd been keeping for her in the entryway and picked up all three as if they weighed nothing.

"I can take one of those," she said before saying more about the favor.

"They aren't heavy. Just lock the door and pull it closed behind us."

Shannon did, returning to the subject of the favor as they went toward her car.

"What if the favor I have to ask is something you'll hate? Shouldn't you hear what it is before you say *sure?*" she teased him, having no idea where the flirtatious tone in her voice had come from.

"I think I can handle whatever you dish out," he flirted back. "What is it?"

As Shannon unlocked the trunk of her car, she said, "When the wedding is over, could you spare some time to go Christmas shopping with me? I bought Chase and Hadley's wedding gift at a store in Billings where they'd registered, but Christmas gifts are different. I thought I might get an idea what to buy after being with them, and then it occurred to me that since you're here and you know everyone better than I do, you'd also know what they might like."

"I could probably do that," Dag said as he put the boxes in the trunk. "We can go on Sunday—ordinarily not all the shops in town are open on Sundays, but this close to Christmas everything is."

"I would be eternally grateful."

"No problem."

And there would be no scheduling conflicts or meetings or public appearances or other obligations that prevented him from accommodating her request—the things that would have kept Wes from doing it at all. Shannon had become so accustomed to Wes putting her off if she did ask something of him that Dag's ready agreement seemed unusual to her.

But she didn't say that. Instead she closed the trunk and headed for the driver's side of the car. Dag managed to reach it at the same time and leaned around her to open her door.

Again she thanked him.

"I'll see you back at Chase and Logan's place," she said then.

"Right behind you," he answered, closing her door with that same big hand pressed to the panel that had been wrapped around hers a few minutes earlier.

That same big hand that her eyes stuck to when he waved it at her and even as it dropped to his jean pocket to dig out his keys.

It had felt so good....

Shannon yanked her thoughts back in line and started her engine, putting her car into gear and heading for the road that led away from the house just ahead of Dag.

Dag, who did stay right behind her all the way home, making it difficult for her to keep from watching him in her rearview mirror.

Dag, who she was thinking about seeing again tonight during the rehearsal dinner.

Dag, who she knew she shouldn't let cloud her thinking at all.

And yet somehow he seemed to be anyway.

Chapter Four

After the wedding rehearsal Friday evening, the dinner was in the poolroom section of a local restaurant and pub called Adz. The pool table had been removed and replaced by dining tables to accommodate what was a large wedding party. The lighting was dim and provided mainly by the candles on each table and there was a roaring fire in a corner fireplace made of rustic stone. The entire place reminded Shannon of an English pub she'd visited on a recent trip to London.

Shannon knew very few people there, and those she did know—Chase and Hadley, Logan and Meg—were busy mingling. Dag was the only other person she knew and he ended up being a godsend because while he was not her formal date to the event, he stayed by her side as if he were, as if he recognized that she was an outsider and had taken it upon himself to make sure she didn't feel that way.

Not that Shannon hadn't become accustomed to being in rooms full of strangers during the past three years. Dating a politician made that a common occurrence and she'd frequently been either expected to stand beside Wes, smile and say nothing, or had been left alone among strangers while Wes glad-handed and networked and basically scoured the crowd for votes or endorsements or funds. But still she appreciated that Dag kept her company. It was a nice change.

And it came in particularly handy when Dag's other brother and sisters headed their way.

"Oh, I'm not going to remember which of your sisters is which," she said quietly to Dag as they approached the spot in front of the fire where Dag and Shannon stood.

"We just wanted to tell you how happy we are that Chase found family," Tucker said as he and his sisters joined them.

Tucker was easy—he was the only other McKendrick male. But even though Shannon had been introduced to the sisters earlier, she'd been introduced to so many people tonight that she couldn't remember which was which.

"I'm happy about it, too," Shannon answered the third McKendrick brother.

"I was just telling Shannon about our names," Dag lied then. "About how with me and the girls, Mom filled in the birth certificates and chose the names when Dad wasn't at the hospital so he wouldn't have a say. How Dad knew the game by the time Tucker was born and made sure he got to pick Tucker's name. But the rest of us—" Dag pointed to each sister as he explained "—Isadora, Theodora and Zeli—those were all Mom."

Shannon was so grateful to him for making that easy for her that she could have hugged him. Instead she just cast him a smile and went along with the ruse that they'd been discussing the names before. "I like unique names, and they give you all something to talk about right off the bat."

"That's true," Zeli agreed with a wry laugh that insinuated that she never got away without talking about her name the minute it was mentioned.

"We all saw you on the news, Shannon," Issa said then. "You looked so shocked—you must not have had any idea that you were going to be proposed to."

"It was a surprise," Shannon agreed, hating that Wes hadn't yet taken her off this hot seat.

"What about a ring, though? You don't have one," Tessa contributed.

"I noticed that, too," Dag commented.

"I'm not a big jewelry person," Shannon said as if the lack of an engagement ring were nothing. Then, desperate not to talk about this, she said, "Speaking of jewelry, Tucker, you did get your cuff links for tomorrow, right? I don't know how they got mixed in with my wedding things, but Chase said he'd get them to you."

"Got 'em," he confirmed. Then, to Dag, he said, "So there was a last-minute change and now I'm walking Tessa down the aisle tomorrow and you're walking Shannon?"

It was news to Shannon that Tucker had ever been set to walk with her and she glanced at Dag to find an expression on his face that said he wasn't pleased that his brother had mentioned this.

"Yeah, I guess it was something to do with height or something," Dag obviously hedged.

"I'm half an inch shorter than you are—how much difference can that make?"

Dag shrugged. "There must be a reason. Maybe for pictures or something. What do I know?"

Shannon couldn't help wondering if Dag had done some backstage rearranging in order to walk with her.

Then with an enormous grin and in a tone that goaded his brother, Tucker said, "Is this another Dag-gets-a-dress-for-Christmas?"

"Oh, cheap shot!" Dag muttered with a laugh.

But that was as far as the confusing exchange went because just then three waitresses bearing dessert trays came into the room and all eyes turned toward them.

"Chocolate Crème Brûlée," Dag announced rather than saying any more to his brother. "Hadley says we're all gonna love this. And you know Hadley knows chocolate."

"She really does," Issa assured Shannon just before Tucker and the sisters moved back to the table they'd all been sharing so they could be served the dessert.

"Looks like that tiny corner booth is empty—what do you say?" Dag suggested then.

They'd had dinner at Hadley and Chase's table, after which everyone had begun to mingle and table-hop. Now some—like Tucker, Issa, Zeli and Tessa—were returning to their original spots, some remained standing and some were taking new seats.

Shannon had no problem with the idea of taking a new seat. In the corner. With Dag.

Not because she wanted to be alone with him, she told herself. But merely because talking to Dag always seemed to come easily, and after a long evening of trying to remember names and relationships and make conversation with a whole lot of people she didn't know, she was more than ready to sit back and relax a little.

"The tiny corner booth it is," she agreed, moving the

few steps required to get there and sliding in from one side just as Dag was waylaid before he could slide in from the other.

Shannon had been introduced to the man who had stopped to talk to Dag and thought she remembered him to be Noah Perry, Meg's brother. He was intent on talking hockey with Dag—a subject that had cropped up several times tonight. Shannon didn't know much about Dag beyond the fact that he was Logan's half brother, but she had gathered here and there that for some reason he had a serious interest in the sport.

But rather than eavesdropping on the conversation the two men were having tableside, Shannon instead fell into studying Dag.

Dress had been decreed casual for the rehearsal and the dinner, so she was wearing charcoal gray pinstripe wool slacks and a white fitted shirt she'd left untucked.

But Dag had gone more casual still. He—and several other men—had on jeans. Dressier jeans than Shannon had seen him in before, jeans that fitted him to a tee, but jeans nonetheless.

And with the jeans he wore a bright pink shirt that he'd taken some ribbing for from Logan and Chase before they'd all left home. But if any man was masculine enough to wear a pink shirt, it was Dag. In fact, somehow the pink shirt topped off by a dark sport coat seemed to lend even more depth to his nearly black eyes, and both shirt and jacket were so expertly tailored that they accentuated the pure massiveness of his shoulders, leaving nothing at all feminine about the way he looked.

Noah Perry didn't keep Dag long and about the time one of the waitresses came to the corner table with the crème brûlées, Dag slid into the booth the way he'd initially intended.

"We need three, Peggy," he told the waitress.

If the teenager wondered why, she didn't ask, she merely left them three of the confections with three spoons and fresh napkins to go with them.

"Hadley isn't the only McKendrick who likes chocolate?" Shannon guessed.

"Maybe I got the extra for you."

"Or maybe you got the extra for you," Shannon countered with a laugh.

"I'll share," he tempted.

"I think I'll be fine with one."

Shannon had cause to rethink that after her first bite of the rich, creamy delicacy lying beneath a crusty shell of caramelized sugar. But she kept her second thoughts to herself even as they agreed that Hadley had made an excellent choice of desserts.

Then Shannon opted for giving Dag a tad more grief and said, "So, between the Dag-gets-a-dress-for-Christmas and the pink shirt, I'm beginning to wonder if there's something I should know about you...."

That made him laugh boisterously. "The shirt is salmon-colored—that's what the sales guy said. Salmon, *not* pink."

Shannon leaned slightly in his direction. "The sales guy lied, it's all pink."

Dag just laughed again. "Hey, I like this shirt."

Shannon did, too, but she didn't tell him that. Or that Wes could never have worn it or been able to look the way Dag did in it.

"And the Dag-gets-a-dress-for-Christmas?" she prompted only because she was curious about his brother's earlier comment. And because she was enjoying giving Dag a hard time.

"That was *me* being a brat as a kid," he answered, referring to her remark that afternoon about herself. "The Christmas I was eight I asked for a fancy dump truck. It had all the bells and whistles—lights that lit up, a switch that made the bed of the truck rise on its own, it even beeped when it backed up. It was great!"

"Uh-huh," Shannon said indulgently.

"I'd been asking for that truck since Thanksgiving and two days before Christmas, Tucker started saying he wanted it, too."

"And you were afraid he would get it and you wouldn't?"

Dag pointed a long, thick index finger at her. "Exactly! My mother was always making me hand something over to Tucker when he asked for it because he was *The Baby*. I figured the truck could be another one of those things, only she'd just give it to him herself."

"You didn't believe in Santa Claus and that Santa would come up with two of them?"

"I was on the fence about Santa by then—you know, hoping he was real, but skeptical. And with the dump truck, I didn't think I could take any chances. It was just that cool," he continued to gush, making Shannon smile as she finished her crème brûlée.

"So what did you do?" she asked, inviting a confession.

Dag had finished his first brûlée, too, and he replaced it with the second, pointing to it with his spoon before he answered her or dug in. "Want to share?"

It was tempting. But Shannon shook her head. "It's so rich—I don't know how you can eat two of them."

"Nothin' to it," he assured.

Then, after cracking the sugar shell to begin his second helping, he went on with his story. "Here's how Christmas was done—presents from Santa weren't wrapped, they were set up and waiting for us. Presents from our parents and other relatives were wrapped. But the presents from our parents never had tags on them. So when we came out in the morning there was a pile for each of us, some with tags from the relatives letting us know which pile was ours."

"And in each pile there were some untagged gifts—I think I'm getting the picture," Shannon said.

"So I snuck out of bed before dawn Christmas morning that year, before any of the other kids, hoping the truck would be set out like a Santa present. But no luck— Tucker and I both had some building blocks and a couple of puzzles—I think—from Santa. Then I checked out all the wrapped packages for Tucker and for me but I couldn't tell what was what—"

"No two were the same?"

"Hey, I was eight, there was no logic to this. Anyway, I found a package in Tucker's pile that I was convinced was the truck. So I took it. Then, in my pea-sized eight-year-old brain, I got the brilliant idea that if I mixed up a few more packages, no one would know I was the one who did it. So I did some of that, never paying any attention to what I was putting where or if I was only switching girls to girls, boys to boys—"

"Oh what a tangled web we weave…" Shannon said with yet another laugh.

"Right."

"And somewhere along the way you ended up with a dress," Shannon concluded, laughing yet again.

Dag made a face. "I think it was called a jumper—it was kind of like a plaid apron with a frilly blouse that went underneath it. Logan encouraged the folks to make me wear it but luckily my dad didn't think that was such a good idea."

Once more Shannon laughed. "Did you get the truck?" she asked sympathetically.

"Tucker and I both got them—in packages I hadn't switched at all. But that was what he was talking about—it's been known ever since as the Dag-gets-a-dress-for-Christmas Christmas."

Funny how Tucker was drawing a comparison between Dag making this secret switch and the change in who was walking her down the aisle tomorrow. So Dag must have done some manipulating to make sure he was her groomsman....

Shannon had no desire to tease him about that. Maybe because she was just pleased that he had done it. Although there certainly wouldn't have been anything wrong with walking with Tucker, she told herself. She was just more familiar now with Dag.

At the head of the room, Logan stood up then to draw everyone's attention. He made a toast to the last night of single life for both Chase and Hadley, joking at their expense before he wished them well and suggested that everyone get home to bed so they could all be well-rested for the wedding the next day.

His advice was unanimously taken and the party broke up.

Shannon had ridden to the church with Chase and Hadley, while Dag had driven his own truck. But because Chase and Hadley were the center of things, when Shannon was ready to go, Chase and Hadley were still saying good-night to people.

"Why don't you just ride with me?" Dag asked with

a nod toward the exit after they'd both put on their coats.

It was late, Shannon was tired and wanted to get things organized for the next day, so she accepted the invitation, ignoring the fact that she just plain liked the idea.

There were still a number of good-nights that had to be said on the way out but they eventually made it to Dag's truck. It was already running and warm when he opened the passenger door to let her in.

"You never left—when did you start this to warm it up?" Shannon marveled.

Dag held up his key ring. "Remote," he said simply. "I did it before we ever stepped foot outside."

"Fancy," Shannon said as she got in, luxuriating in the warmth.

When Dag rounded the rear of the truck and slipped in behind the wheel, she said, "You don't worry about somebody stealing your car when they walk by and see it running with no one in it?"

"First of all, the doors have to be locked for the remote to work, and I have to have another key to open them. But even if that wasn't true, we're in Northbridge—everybody knows everybody, everybody knows everybody's car or truck—no one could drive off in something they didn't own and get away with it."

"There *is* a lot of everybody-knows-everybody, isn't there?" Shannon said as Dag headed for home. "I couldn't keep all the Perrys and Pratts and Walkers and Grants and Graysons straight."

"The Graysons are actually new to Northbridge, but since they married the Perrys and a Pratt, I can see where it would still get confusing. It's good, though, like being one big—for the most part happy—family."

"And you know them all?"

"Eventually you get to know them all, even the ones who move in. It's just that kind of community."

"Did you like growing up here?" she asked because she could tell that he honestly was happy in his old hometown.

"I know—you grew up in Billings and still felt like your life was small, so you figure growing up in a small town must have been *ree-eally* claustrophobic. But it wasn't. I loved it. I mean, my mom was kind of a pain, but other than that? I had more freedom than you probably did growing up in the city. I pretty much came and went as I pleased as long as I checked in every couple of hours."

Shannon glanced over at his profile, finding it impossible not to admire despite a slight bump on the bridge of his nose that she'd never noticed before. "What did you do with that freedom?" she asked.

"Anything I could think of," he said with a nostalgic shake of his head, as if the mere memory transported him to the heart of the fun he'd had. "Summers I'd hop on my bike—even after dark—find my friends and we'd just hang out or walk Main Street or play baseball or go to whatever event was happening at the town square, or have ice cream or swim or get into mischief—"

"Innocent mischief?"

He shot her a sideways glance that went with a grin full of devilry. "Sure," he said as if there was no chance that he would admit to anything else.

Then he went on with his answer about what he'd done with his freedom as a kid. "In the fall there was Halloween, and Northbridge loves its holidays. The whole town gets into the act, so that was great. Trick or treating was an endurance sport because the only boundaries were the city limits. It's beautiful around here when the leaves fall—we'd rake them up and jump in them or have bonfires. Sometimes we'd go hunting—"

"Mischief-makers with guns?" Shannon said in mock horror.

He just smiled at her again and went on. "Winter was ice skating and sledding and skiing and snowball fights and snow forts. And spring—well, not only is school gonna end and summer is coming, but before that there's mud-month. For a kid, sliding through it, sloshing around in it, wrestling in it, having tugs-of-war over the worst puddles of it? Heaven…"

Shannon laughed at his rapture. "It does sound like you had a good time."

"The best," he confirmed as he pulled off the main road and drove past Logan and Meg's house to come to a stop at the garage below the apartment where Shannon was staying.

Shannon didn't wait for him to come around and open her door, and they both got out of the truck at the same time. But while she was reminding herself that this was merely one person giving another person a ride home, that it was *not* a date, still when she headed for the stairs on the side of the garage, Dag tagged along to walk her to her door as if it were.

"Am I wrong or for you is tomorrow an all-day-getting-ready-for-this-thing thing?" Dag asked along the way.

"A group hair appointment will go from early in the morning until early in the afternoon. Then there's makeup and dressing, and getting to the church for the seven o'clock ceremony. So you're right, for those of us on the female side of the wedding, tomorrow is an all-day-getting-ready-for-this-thing thing. It takes a lot to do a big wedding."

"For the guys, not so much. My day looks like the way today was—I'm working at the house, I'll come home, shower, shave and dress. The only difference will be the tux. And I think tomorrow night we're all meeting for a better pre-festivities drink—tonight we had a beer. I understand Chase has some premium scotch we're breaking out tomorrow night to kick things off."

"Oh, yeah, much easier to be a guy," Shannon said as she opened the apartment door.

She didn't go in, however; she stayed on the landing as Dag said, "So I guess the next time I see you it will be at the church."

"I will not be the one in the white dress," Shannon joked because there was an odd tone to Dag's voice that almost made it seem as if he thought not seeing her again until the next evening was too long a time to wait. And even though she told herself she must be mistaken, she wasn't quite sure how to respond.

"Oh, I think I'll be able to pick you out of the crowd anyway," he said in a completely different tone of voice— that one somehow intimate and tantalizing.

They were facing each other and Dag was peering intently down at her, but Shannon took a more concentrated look at him to try to tell if she was imagining things. What she found was a small smile curling the corners of his mouth. And she felt her own gaze inexplicably drawn to that mouth, to those sexy roller-coaster lips that she suddenly couldn't help yearning to feel pressed to hers...

Would they be as soft and warm as they looked? As supple? What kind of kisser was he? Not pinch-lipped the way Wes sometimes was, she thought. Relaxed, confident, natural—that was Dag and probably how Dag kissed....

But that wasn't anything she should be thinking about! she reprimanded herself.

She jerked her eyes away from their study of his mouth just about the time Dag said more to himself than to her, "Engaged...to a Rumson..."

Would he have kissed her otherwise? Shannon wondered. Was that what he'd been thinking about, too?

Her strongest sense was that it was.

But that still didn't make it okay, she told herself. She was moving on with her life after this holiday and that could well mean Beverly Hills. She couldn't start anything with Dag that would only end when Christmas was over.

Which meant that maybe Dag believing that she was engaged was sort of a safety net for her.

"Okay, then," he said suddenly, firmly, taking the top step backward. "I guess I'll see you tomorrow night."

"Thanks for the ride home," Shannon answered as if nothing else at all had passed between them. Because it actually hadn't, regardless of the fact that it felt as if something had.

"No problem," he assured, turning to descend the rest of the steps with his back to her. "Night."

"Night," Shannon called as she went into the apartment and closed the door between them.

But as she deflated against it, she couldn't help feeling a tiny bit more perturbed with Wes than she had been.

Because if Wes had publicly set her free before tonight, Dag might have kissed her.

And while she knew it was better that that hadn't happened, she was still dying to know what it might have been like if he had.

Chapter Five

Shannon ended up enjoying Saturday's wedding preparations more than she'd anticipated. Although she was a stranger among the other women who made up the bridal party and had the lifelong connection of Northbridge, there was nothing in the way they treated her that would indicate otherwise. They made her feel like one of the group—one of the family, actually—and it turned out to be a lot of fun to be included in the hair and makeup sessions, and in the general preparations for the wedding.

The seven o'clock ceremony was held at the local church that served all denominations. Hadley had kept with a Christmas theme. White candles and tiny white lights illuminated the church, which was adorned with red roses, sprigs of holly and holly berries intermingled with baby's breath flowers.

Because Hadley was a seamstress with a background

in dress design, and had worked in haute couture in both Italy and France for many years, she'd designed her own gown and those of her bridesmaids and flower girl. With the help of a local seamstress, she had also made the dresses. Hadley's wedding gown was simple white satin with a fitted, strapless bodice and a full floor-length skirt in front that gracefully elongated in back to a five-foot train. A red sash marked her waist and tied in a large bow at the base of her spine, then fell in two long streamers that matched the length of the train.

Tia was the flower girl and her dress was similar to the bride's—it was also white, though white organza rather than satin. It had short puffy sleeves like two clouds billowing from each shoulder, and an empire waist wrapped with a red-and-white polka-dot sash and a bow that tied in front.

Each of the seven bridesmaids' dresses were fashioned in styles to make the women who would wear them feel comfortable and to best accentuate their own personal body sizes and shapes. But all were made of red organza and dropped to just below knee-length.

Shannon's dress was a formfitting halter with a deceptively high collar that wrapped her neck but completely exposed her back. For the ceremony she wore a matching shrug that made the ensemble seem more conservative. But for the reception she had the option of removing the short jacket and exposing a dress that looked classic from the front and sexy from behind.

The wedding ceremony itself was traditional and touching, especially when Chase and Hadley had their turn at saying a few words about what they meant to the other and how happy they were to have come full circle from their childhood acquaintance to find each other now.

And when their vows had been exchanged and they were pronounced man and wife, the church bells were rung.

Then the reception was held in the showroom portion of Mackey and McKendrick Furniture Designs. The furniture showcases had been emptied for the occasion, allowing room for the buffet table, the eight-man band, a dance floor and dozens of red-and-white-linen covered dining tables and chairs along the perimeter.

In the center of each dining table was a pyramid of small, festively wrapped boxes that each held a piece of Belgian chocolate in the shape of a wedding cake as special treats for all the guests.

Shannon had volunteered to care for her nephew during the reception and to babysit overnight, as well, when Chase and Hadley would take their one-night honeymoon in a countryside cabin far on the outskirts of Northbridge. Also, since she hadn't thought there would be much mingling to do, she'd offered to watch Logan and Meg's three-year-old daughter, Tia, in thanks for their hospitality. When Tia had learned that Shannon was spending the night with Cody, Tia hadn't wanted to be left out, so as a result, the three-year-old was sleeping over at Chase and Hadley's loft tonight, too.

All of which Shannon had felt just fine about. But what she hadn't considered was that although she was a virtual stranger to Northbridge, her grandmother had lived all of her adult life there, and that everyone who had known Carol Duffy might choose the wedding as an opportunity to say hello, to give their condolences to Shannon, to talk a little about her grandmother. So Shannon found herself juggling a fifteen-month-old who had only recently discovered his own mobility and wanted to exercise it rather than be contained and a precocious three-year-old, while doing far more socializing than she'd bargained for.

Had Dag not taken it upon himself to stay by her side the entire time, it might have been far worse. But as it was, not only had he apparently assigned himself to be her groomsman when it came to walking her down the aisle, but he stayed with her and the kids for the reception, as well. Which also helped tremendously when other guests approached her about her grandmother because Dag knew them all, introduced them and filled any gaps.

"I am sooo going to owe you," Shannon told him after he'd provided that service for about the dozenth time.

"Yeah, you are," he agreed before he said, "For what?"

"I thought I'd be sitting alone in a corner so I might as well take Cody and Tia just for company. But tonight hasn't been anything like that. I don't think I could have done it without you."

And to prove her point, Cody chose that moment to climb from Shannon's lap onto the table and very nearly knock over a full glass of water. But Dag caught the glass just in time.

"*I* thought I might get at least one dance with you," Dag countered. "But it doesn't look like that's gonna happen, so I was thinking that now that the cake is cut, maybe we ought to snag a few pieces, take these two upstairs to the loft to eat it—so we don't end up with cake on the floor, too—and then put them to bed."

A dish of appetizers and Tia's chicken had been knocked off the table by the kids and, like Dag, Shannon wasn't looking forward to cake being the next course to hit the floor. And it was more than an hour after Tia's bedtime and more than two hours later than Cody usually went down for the night. Plus Shannon had not thought she would have any help getting the duo to bed, but if Dag was volunteering…

Still, she felt obligated to give him an out. "I'm the one who signed on for babysitting duty. Are you sure you don't want to stay down here and enjoy the rest of the night the way everyone else is?"

He smiled. "Who says I won't enjoy the rest of the night if I go upstairs?"

There was a lascivious sound to that that Dag must have realized only after he'd said it because his smile stretched into a grin and he added, "I've had about enough of the wedding stuff anyway. Getting out of this noise, away from all these people to eat cake in some peace and quiet, and then listen to you read Tia *Good-night Moon*—what could be better than that? Besides, if I stay down here I'll just end up dancing with my sisters."

"Okay, then, I'm not dumb enough to turn down an offer of help with these two," Shannon said, knowing she probably should just because she liked the idea of Dag's continued help and company more than she had any business liking it.

But that was all the encouragement he needed to stand and say, "I'll get the cake and we can go."

Chase and Hadley were occupied, but while Dag was gone Shannon caught Meg's attention and motioned her to the table to tell Meg the plan.

Meg agreed that it was long past the bedtimes of both kids. She asked Shannon if Shannon was sure she didn't mind leaving, and when Shannon insisted she didn't, Meg kissed both children good-night, said she'd let Logan, Chase and Hadley know what was going on, and turned to leave just as Dag came back to the table with the slices of cake.

"Thanks for lending Shannon a hand," Meg said as they crossed paths.

"Glad to do it," Dag assured, and something about that made Meg smile knowingly as she moved off to rejoin the festivities.

"All set?" Dag asked then.

"All set," Shannon answered.

Tia was tired and beginning to be cranky and unco-operative so she let it be known she didn't want to leave. Shannon used the promise of cake to lure her into compliance, and with Cody slung on one of Shannon's hips, the three-year-old finally accepted Shannon's free hand and allowed herself to be led through the celebration to the workroom and up the stairs that led from there to Chase and Hadley's loft.

"Let's do pajamas first and then have cake—cake always tastes better in pajamas," Shannon said when they were upstairs.

"Are you and Uncle Dag gonna put on your 'jamas, too?" Tia asked.

"Good question," Dag said under his breath, laughing at what Shannon had unwittingly walked into.

"No, cake just tastes better for kids when the kids are in their pajamas," Shannon improvised.

Tia frowned as if that didn't make sense but before she could pursue anything more along those lines, Dag again saved the day and said, "So, shall we split up boys and girls? I'll get Cody ready for bed and Shannon, you can get Tia out of that dress she looked so pretty in tonight."

As if on cue, Tia swirled around to make the skirt billow out—something she'd done numerous times during the evening.

"Cody will need a diaper change, you know…" Shannon reminded Dag.

"Yeah, no big deal. I've done it before."

"Then its boys with boys, girls with girls," Shannon agreed. "Tia's things are in Chase and Hadley's room with mine so you and Cody can have the nursery to yourselves, and we'll meet back here for cake when we're finished."

"Deal," Dag decreed, setting the plates full of cake on the island counter and taking Cody from Shannon's arms. "Come on, little man, you don't look like you're gonna last too much longer."

In the end, Cody didn't stay awake long enough for the cake—when Dag joined Shannon and the pajama-clad Tia in the kitchen portion of the loft again, he announced that Cody had fallen asleep on the changing table. "So I just put him in his crib."

"Tha's cuz Cody's a big baby—he can't stay awake and he gots to sleep in a crib, and he calls his moose *oose*," Tia said as if she were far above that.

"You call your gorilla *grilla*. And before you know it, Cody will be keeping up with you just fine, Miss Tia. He's no better or worse than you, and you're no better or worse than he is," Dag said as Shannon poured the little girl a glass of milk.

Shannon studied the frown that went with the gentle reprimand from Dag as she returned to the island counter where Tia was sitting with her cake in front of her.

"A lecture on equality?" Shannon said quietly to him.

"Sore point with me."

Shannon didn't push it with Tia there and Tia didn't

seem to notice anything because she was more interested in why Shannon and Dag had opted to have their cake later.

When Tia was finished with her piece—and indulged by her uncle with a few bites of Cody's piece—Shannon washed Tia's face, helped Tia brush her teeth and together she and Dag read the bedtime story Tia required before she slipped off to sleep in Chase and Hadley's big bed.

But when Shannon and Dag returned to the island counter to stand on opposite sides of it and eat their cake, Shannon said, "Tia's pseudo-sibling-rivalry with Cody bothers you?"

"It isn't that. It's that hint of superiority that came with it tonight. After years of my mother thinking she was better than everybody and putting on airs, it sort of pushes my buttons when anyone does it."

"The putting-on-airs thing—you really didn't like that about her.…"

"I really didn't. Don't get me wrong, I loved my mother, she was a decent enough mom…well, not to Logan and Hadley, she resented having stepkids and let them know it—"

"Chase told me a little about that—Hadley found comfort in food and ended up being very overweight until she got away from your mother, is the way I understood it."

"That's true—poor Hadley took the brunt of my mother's mean streak."

"But to you, Tucker, Issa, Zeli and Tessa—"

"She was okay. She kind of left us alone while she put all her energy into trying to dress fancier than everyone else, trying to talk more formally, trying to make sure our house, our car, everything about us put other people to shame. Not that any of it made her happy, because it didn't—"

"It seems like it would have made her isolated."

"Exactly! She alienated everyone with her I'm-better-than-you-are attitude. She wouldn't *lower herself to the level of the peons*—as she said—but that meant she didn't have any friends, any outlets, she never enjoyed anything because it didn't meet her high standards. It made her difficult to like and there was no living with it without being affected by it."

"Did she just not want to be in Northbridge?"

"She said that it was too dull and ordinary for her. But there wasn't anywhere else she wanted to be, either—my father killed himself trying to find any way to please her and there were half a dozen times when he said he'd pack us all up and move anywhere she wanted to go—"

"*That* must have been scary—moves are so unsettling for kids."

"Oh, yeah, it worried me every time that she was going to take him up on it and we'd all have to leave our friends, our school, our home—"

"But she didn't."

"To tell you the truth, I think Northbridge was tailor-made for her. Finding fault in the simplicity of the town, in the fact that the people who live here are so down-to-earth, was how she elevated herself. So no, she didn't ever take my dad up on his offer to leave. I think here she could think of herself as the big fish in the little pond, and she definitely didn't want to be the little fish in the big pond."

"So you don't think she just wanted more out of life?"

"Like you do?"

"Do I *put on airs?*" Shannon asked, alarmed that he might think that of her.

He smiled as if her concern entertained him. "Not that I've noticed. But you did say you've always wanted a bigger life than your parents had."

"True. But it's the life I want to be bigger. I still want to be me."

"I hope so, because you're pretty good," he complimented with another smile—this one appreciative enough to send a warm rush through her as she finished her cake and watched Dag polish off what was left of the piece Cody hadn't eaten.

Then Dag continued with what they were talking about. "I think there's something to be said for people who can be happy with who they are, with what they have, who can make the best of the cards life deals them. It sounds like that's what your parents did and you admired them for it."

"I guess that's true—that was how my parents were and I did admire them for it," Shannon agreed. "But maybe some people need more and there's nothing wrong with trying to achieve that, either."

Shannon couldn't be sure whether the music from the reception downstairs suddenly got louder, or with the kids asleep and the silence that followed that last statement, it just seemed that way.

Dag must have noticed it, too. He'd been leaning on the island counter and just then he straightened up, looking as if something had just occurred to him. "Hey, maybe I can have that dance with you after all."

"Here? Now?"

"Why not? There's music—not loud, but there's still music. There's an open area, there's a hardwood floor..."

The loft did have a lot of open areas, particularly just a few feet from where they were, in front of an entire wall of windows where stars sparkled in the sky overhead and the main house in the distance was brilliantly and colorfully illuminated with Christmas lights.

"Come on, dance with me—you would if we were downstairs, wouldn't you?"

She probably would have, yes. Just to be polite…

"Come on," Dag repeated, clasping her hand in his to bring her out from behind the counter and with him to that spot near the windows.

When they got there he used a bit of a flourish to spin her into his arms where his other hand landed on her bare back and sent a wholly pleasant little shiver up her spine.

It's just a dance, she told herself. *An innocent little dance like everyone downstairs is doing…*

And yet this seemed so much more intimate. Especially since she was ultra-aware of the feel of Dag's skin pressed to hers.

She tried not to focus on that, though, as she fell into step with him.

"You're a good dancer," she said with some surprise. And with a secret wish that he wasn't quite as good as he was—if he hadn't been, maybe he wouldn't have been able to keep such a respectable space between them. "I haven't run into many men who can dance at all, let alone well."

"You can't be talking about your Rumson—"

"Wes can dance—all the Rumsons learn how early because dancing at fancy dress balls and parties and at their country club makes for good photo opportunities," she said, reiterating what Wes had told her. "But when it comes to non-Rumsons—"

"I didn't have to learn to dance for photo opportunities, but it *was* part of my mother's notions of high society—she said that all people of class knew how to dance. And the girls had to wear party dresses and the boys had to be in a suit and tie so we learned the *correct comportment.*"

That explained the respectable space between them.

But once the wedding pictures had all been taken, Dag had removed his bow tie and cummerbund. His tuxedo jacket had come off by the time dinner was served. The collar button of his pleated white shirt was unfastened, and he was definitely looking like himself—in what was left of the tux, he'd managed to combine refined and relaxed. So Shannon wouldn't have minded it if he had eased up a little on that comportment, too, to hold her closer.

But instead he displayed what he'd probably also been taught—to make polite conversation while dancing.

"So, kindergarten, huh? You start at the ground floor with the kiddos?"

"Actually, for most kids the ground floor is preschool now. But yes, I teach kindergarten."

"Kindergarten for me was more playtime than learning."

"Playtime teaches kids social skills and to share and to cooperate with other kids—there's value in it. But there are academics now, too—work on reading and writing, numbers, the basics."

"Ah, I'm underestimating the kindergarten teacher of today—it's not just sing-alongs and reading stories and breaking up fights over toys?"

"There's all that, too, but there's also definitely more to it than that."

"And why did you pick the beginners rather than say... fourth grade?"

Had he just adjusted his hand on her back and brought her the tiniest bit nearer?

Shannon had to tip up her head slightly more to peer into that handsome face, so she thought he might have.

Not that she was inclined to complain...

"I'm licensed to teach K through sixth, but I like the really little kids," she answered his question. "They're so full of life and so unjaded. They truly believe the world is their oyster, that anything—and everything—is possible. I guess I like to believe that, too. And seeing things through a kindergartner's eyes helps."

Dag was looking down into *her* eyes and that explanation seemed to please him because he smiled an appreciative smile. "You're good with Tia and Cody. And Tia is crazy about you. So I'm betting that teaching is what you're cut out for."

"I never doubted it. Even now, when I've needed time off and appreciated having it, I've still missed my job."

"Are you going back to work after Christmas break?"

"No, actually I'm going to Beverly Hills."

"California?" he said with an arch of his eyebrows.

"I have a good friend there—Dani Bond. She's been my best friend since first grade, we were college roommates. She married a businessman from Beverly Hills and she's building her own private school...well, with the help of her husband's funding. The Early Childhood Development Center."

"Fancy. And private, I'll bet."

"Yes, private. And intended to attract the Beverly Hills elite. Dani will make sure that it also provides the best possible early education and academic foundation for kids from pre-kindergarten through sixth grade." Without thinking, Shannon added, "She wants me in on it with her. She's invited me to invest the money from selling my parents' business and the building it was in, and from Gramma's house, to be a partner in the school. I could head the pre-K and kindergarten portion and teach, too."

"Wow. That sounds exciting. But how does that fit in with marrying Wes Rumson and potentially becoming Montana's First Lady?"

Oh, for a minute she'd forgotten.

Shannon could have kicked herself.

It was just *too* easy to talk to this man.

And too easy to forget herself and everything else she should be remembering.

"Well, sure…I mean…I couldn't do both…at least not the work parts. I could still invest in Dani's school," she said haltingly as she stumbled to keep the secret of her nonexistent engagement. "Anyway, you asked if I was going back to work after Christmas and I'm not. I have plans to visit Dani, to check things out, to see what I think. Right now I'm just considering what to do."

Dag went on studying her for a long moment as they continued to dance, and Shannon had the sense that she was being read like a book.

Then he proved her right when he said, "So, really, you have your choice of two lives bigger than what you've known. You're engaged to a Rumson who will likely be the next Governor. Or you could invest in your friend's school, be instrumental in setting the educational foundation of kids of the rich and famous, and make your own flashier life—"

Dag definitely saw things too clearly.

"Wes says I'd just be wiping their noses," Shannon heard herself say before she even knew she was going to, appreciating that Dag's view of her opportunity was not so pompous.

But she knew she'd ventured further than she should have already and she needed to rectify it, so she shrugged and said, "It's just the investment opportunity I'm checking out after Christmas."

Dag nodded but she didn't think he completely believed her.

Before he could pursue it, though, the bandleader's voice came over the muffled strains of music to announce that the next song would be the last.

"We better make this good," Dag said as the band segued into a romantic ballad.

That was when comportment finally went out the window.

In keeping with custom, Shannon's right hand was in Dag's left. He raised her hand to his shoulder and let it rest there in order to clasp both of his hands at the small of her back in a very informal—and even more intimate—dance posture. He also closed that respectable space between them completely by pulling her near enough for their bodies to touch, for Shannon to have no choice but to put her cheek to the rock-hard wall of his chest while her other hand pressed to the expanse of his broad shoulders.

"Wouldn't your mother be upset with your *comportment?*" Shannon whispered.

She half expected him to say *Wouldn't your fiancé have a fit if he knew you were letting me do this?*

But the only sound Dag made was a soft response into her hair. "Shhh…I won't tell if you won't."

Shannon knew that if she truly had been engaged,

she probably shouldn't have gone along with this. But his arms were strong around her, bracketing hers like muscular parentheses. He smelled of a fresh, citrusy cologne. His body was big and warm and powerful. And it was just all too nice to deny herself what she continued to insist was nothing more than a dance. A simple, harmless dance...

A dance that really just amounted to swaying in place now...

Then the music ended and the distant voice from below congratulated Chase and Hadley one last time and wished them well.

And while Shannon regretted it, Dag stopped their dancing on cue, too, and released his hold of her enough for there to be a separation between them again. Enough for his arms to only be loosely around her still as he smiled down at her.

"Sooo much better than dancing with my sisters," he said in a deep, quiet voice.

Shannon returned his smile, looking up into his thickly lashed, almost-black eyes as they peered down into hers.

And for no reason it just seemed like a moment for him to kiss her.

*Go ahead...*she silently urged, wanting him to, unable to convince herself it was a bad idea even though she tried.

And she thought he might do it because his chin tipped downward just slightly, because his gaze went from her eyes to her lips, because she even found her own chin raising a fraction of an inch to encourage him.

But then those brawny shoulders of his drew back enough to break the spell that dancing seemed to have cast, and as he pulled his arms from around her, he instead caught her hand again.

It was that hand that he brought up to his lips, pressing them to the back of it, kissing it very gallantly before he released it and said, "I suppose I should go see if I'm needed to get things wrapped up down there."

Shannon nodded her agreement with that and walked him to the top of the stairs that would take him back to the workroom, silently swearing to herself that the kiss on the hand had been more than sufficient....

"Thanks for everything tonight," she said when they reached the doorway that opened to the steps.

"Don't mention it. And tomorrow we're going Christmas shopping, right?"

"I feel kind of guilty asking more of you after all this."

"I'm looking forward to it," he said sincerely. Then he leaned forward and added, "Just don't tell your Rumson and get my butt kicked."

"Believe me, you don't have to worry about that," she said wryly.

"I'll see you tomorrow, then."

Can't wait, she thought.

But she didn't say it.

She merely nodded and, after exchanging good-nights, watched him go down the stairs.

Then she turned and headed for the bedrooms to check on the kids.

And somehow along the way she discovered herself staring at the back of that hand Dag had kissed.

And recalling every detail of how his lips had felt there.

And really, really wishing—in spite of everything—that she'd felt those lips on her own instead.

Chapter Six

Shannon spent Sunday morning with Cody and Tia, and it started her day off just right. Her hiatus from teaching had left a shortage of kid contact in her life and since that was something that genuinely uplifted her, she drank in every moment with the duo until Meg and Logan came to the apartment to take Tia off her hands, and—a while after that—Chase and Hadley returned from their one-night honeymoon to get Cody.

Then Shannon and Dag were off to shop down North-bridge's Main Street.

Prior to that afternoon, Shannon hadn't taken full notice of just how thoroughly—and splendidly—the small town celebrated the Christmas holiday. But there was no overlooking it in the heart of things on the last weekend before Christmas.

In the cold, crisp winter air every building front was outlined in lights that were turned on to brighten the overcast threat of the storm that was coming. Every eave had both real and decorative icicles hanging from them like glittery crystal spears. Every door had a wreath, and every display window had a Christmas scene or Christmas wares exhibited.

Lining the sidewalk were Victorian-style wrought iron streetlights all wrapped in tiny white lights, pine boughs and red ribbons that were also strung between them like a canopy.

At the corners of each of the three cross streets, there were decorated Christmas trees. And for Sunday there were numerous carts selling ornaments, trinkets and gift items; warm, salty pretzels; mulled cider and hot chocolate; sugar-and-spice almonds; popcorn; roasted chestnuts; and cookies, fudge and divinity aplenty.

There were also carolers outside the general merchandise store whose songs echoed the full length of Main, and a Santa Claus—who *wasn't* Dag—set up at the end of a candy-cane-lined walkway that led to the courthouse doors. He sat on a red velvet throne waiting to hear children's requests.

All in all, Shannon thought it was like a scene from a Dickens novel except there wasn't a Scrooge to be seen, and she again found only warmth and welcome and people who seemed to feel she was one of the local family even though she was basically a stranger to them.

Dag came through for her with gift suggestions. For Meg and Hadley she bought copies of a book he said they were both dying to read. For Logan there was an autographed baseball that Dag said his brother had been admiring in a store window since it had appeared there. And Chase's gift was also a gift to herself and the other brothers she still hadn't found—four family albums and Shannon's promise to fill them with photographs that would give the separated siblings a sense of their years growing up apart and then continue with photos from now.

"I know you probably haven't had time yet to go through the stuff from the house—"

"I haven't even taken the boxes out of the trunk of my car," Shannon told Dag when he recommended the albums.

"—but there are about five old pictures I came across stuck in the back of a drawer and four of them are of you as a kid. If you can part with three of them, you could start the albums with those."

Shannon thought it was a great idea.

Gifts for Tia and Cody were more plentiful just because Shannon couldn't resist a few indulgences during their hour in the toy store. Plus the kids were also getting books, though Dag said he'd yet to hear of Tia sitting still for anything but *Goodnight Moon.*

During the course of the afternoon, Dag also finished his Christmas shopping and for a short while at the end of the day, they parted at Shannon's request so she could retrace her steps slightly and buy Dag a sweater he'd considered buying himself and then hadn't.

It was cashmere and probably more than she should have spent on him. But she rationalized that besides being something she knew he liked, she owed him for all he'd done to keep her company through the wedding, for shopping with her today and for sharing gift ideas that were insightful and had made for presents that she was looking forward to giving on Christmas morning.

And when he'd held up the sweater in front of him, the deep charcoal-gray color had emphasized his dark coloring and made him look indescribably dashing, and she'd known at that moment that she just had to see him wearing it. Extravagant or not.

As dusk fell they could have gone home but Dag had a better idea—a dinner of pizza and beer to get them off their feet for a little while, then some ice skating in the town square where Shannon had first seen him.

"I'll call home and tell them to eat without us," he said, and like his other suggestions, it had too much appeal for her to reject.

So pizza and beer it was, sitting at the front window of the local pizzeria.

"Look at that," Dag said as he peered out at the beauty of Main Street while they ate.

Shannon was looking at something, but it wasn't out the window. She was looking at him, dressed in jeans and a plaid flannel shirt over a Henley T-shirt—all outdoorsy and wintery, his heavy five o'clock shadow making him look very rugged and handsome.

"It's like a postcard out there," Dag added, forcing Shannon to amend her gaze to take in what he was marveling at.

He was right, but it was his awe-filled admiration of his hometown that made Shannon smile. Well, that and just how much she liked the way his face was lined with pleasure.

"You really love it here," she said.

"There's nowhere else I want to be."

"I don't really know much about your background," she said then, when his appreciation for Northbridge struck her as somewhat curious. "I know you grew up here, but it seems like you've moved around as an adult. And since you just bought Gramma's house, I guess I assumed you've lived somewhere else until now, that you're just moving back. If you love Northbridge so much, why *haven't* you always lived here?"

"It was the hockey—no team in Northbridge," he said simply. And as if she should know what he was talking about.

"I've figured out that you *like* hockey," she said, confused. "But you wouldn't live here just because there isn't a team?"

Something seemed to strike him suddenly and he smiled a wide smile. "I played hockey. I played hockey to get me through college and then I played it professionally in Detroit."

It took a moment for that to sink in, for Shannon to put two and two together. In all the mentions of Dag and hockey, there had never been anything about him playing *professionally*. She'd thought that it was a passion of his, that he'd probably played in school, that maybe he played recreationally, the way Wes golfed. It had never occurred to her that hockey had been Dag's *career*.

"Seriously?" she said. "You were a professional hockey player?"

"Past tense. I suppose I thought you knew because everyone around here does. Everyone who knows me knows. And…well, a lot of people know—it's the kind of thing that's…well…known…."

"You're a celebrity and I completely missed it?" Shannon exclaimed with a laugh.

Dag grimaced. "Not really a *celebrity*. But making a living at a professional sport is kind of a public occupation. And my career ended with a splash, so most of the time, people know I played hockey for a living without my telling them."

"I didn't," Shannon confessed. "I've never been interested in any sport. Or who plays. I completely stop paying attention to anything that comes up that has to do with sports. I'm sorry."

"Nothing to be sorry about."

"When did you stop playing?"

"About this time two years ago." But rather than go on with that, he returned to the original topic. "So, no, I haven't lived in Northbridge since I left for college—"

"Where you also played hockey—"

"On a full scholarship to the University of North Dakota—go Fighting Sioux!" he said in a joking cheer. "Then the Red Wings signed me so I moved to Michigan. I came back to Northbridge for extended visits whenever I could during the off-season, but that's all it's been—visits."

"And you missed it?"

"Oh, yeah! Not only is Northbridge home, but there's just something about it that you don't find in other places. It's like this secret safe haven from the rest of the world."

"Bad things never happen here?" Shannon teased him because he was so over-the-top about this place.

"Sure, bad things happen everywhere. But when they happen here, you're never alone with it. Everyone jumps in and does whatever they can to help. You're a prime example of that—when your folks were killed in that car wreck, the cops brought you to Meg's grandfather, the reverend. He let word out that there were kids who needed homes and slam-bam-thank-you-ma'am, you got homes."

"Chase didn't."

"No, Chase sort of fell through the cracks on that score. But he did grow up here and even though his foster father was a jerk, Chase still came away from Northbridge liking it enough to move back."

There was no disputing that.

"Northbridge is…" Dag shrugged as if it was difficult to sum up. "It's the kind of place where I know when I first start to farm, to ranch this spring, every other farmer, every other rancher around here will be willing to lend me a hand if I need it, to share his or her secrets—well, most of them anyway. Butch Butler will never tell anybody what he's feeding that prize pig of his. But you get the picture. Plus there's this—"

He motioned toward the window.

"Every city and town decorates for Christmas," Shannon pointed out.

"It isn't the decorations, it's everything that goes with it—the spirit of things, the way everyone gets into this holiday and all the rest. The way a wedding or a new baby is happy, important news no matter whose family it is. The way people around here just *care*. I like that."

"Family, team sports, this town—I think there's a theme with you," Shannon said.

Dag laughed. "I hadn't thought about it like that, but you're right—I am *not* a loner. I like being a part of a close-knit group that's working and playing together."

Once they'd finished eating, their waitress appeared tableside to ask if they'd like anything else. When they said no, she set down the bill and two complimentary cookies that looked like small frosted knots.

"The owner's aunt makes these cookies at Christmas—they're Italian anise knots. I love them, they taste like licorice," Dag explained as he paid the bill.

They ate the cookies as they moved on to the town square where the gazebo was completely lit by tiny white lights. All the fir trees were decorated and lit up, too. More Victorian-style streetlights lined the outer perimeter of the square and had strings of the bough-

and-ribbon-wrapped lights draped between them to il-luminate the entire area.

Before dinner they had stopped at Dag's truck to leave their day's purchases and to get his ice skates. Now Shannon rented a pair for herself from a stand by the rink.

"It doesn't matter—because I can teach you—but do you ice skate?" Dag asked as they sat on the benches that lined the ice just inside the decorated railing.

"I used to," Shannon said. "I haven't since I was a teenager, and even then I preferred wheels to blades."

"You'll have to come back in the summer, then—when the ice melts, there's roller skating and skateboarding here."

Shannon was perplexed by why that should have any appeal at all, but it did. She didn't respond, though, and once their skates were in place, Dag got up onto his first. Then he spun around to face her and hold out his hands to help her get to her feet.

"You're just assuming I'm going to be a klutz?" she joked.

His only answer was an engaging grin while his hands remained outstretched to her, waiting to be taken.

They both had on gloves so she thought it was safe enough to accept his help. But even through two layers of knitted wool just the meeting of their hands sent a warmth all through her.

But it only lasted a moment because she had to concentrate on maintaining her precarious balance.

"It's been a *very* long time since I was on skates," she said, stating the obvious.

"Yeah, you're a little wobbly, but you'll get the feel for it again," Dag said as he steadied her and began to skate backward to tow her out onto the ice at a snail's pace.

He was right, it didn't take Shannon long to regain the knack of ice skating. But once that happened, even when Dag let go of her and turned to skate at her side, she was no match for him. He glided so effortlessly across the ice that there were times as they circled the rink with the rest of the skaters that Shannon glanced down to make sure he wasn't just floating.

But she didn't mind that he was better than she was. There was Christmas music playing over a speaker system, there were lots of people laughing and enjoying themselves—despite a few spills on the ice here and there—and there were kids galore.

And if Shannon hadn't just found out over dinner that Dag had played professional hockey, she would have discovered it then because many of those kids—as well as a few of the adults—seemed awestruck to be seeing Dag on the ice. They mentioned games and plays in which he'd apparently dazzled them.

But in spite of the friendliness and the adulation, Dag was all hers. He answered whatever greeting or question or comment was aimed at him, he introduced her whenever the opportunity arose, but nothing and no one ever took him from her side or kept his primary focus from her.

They skated for about an hour before the cold seeped through Shannon's wool coat and earmuffs, through the crewneck sweater she was wearing, through the turtleneck that was underneath the sweater, even through her jeans.

Dag didn't appear as affected as she was, but before she had found the words to tell him that she was freezing, he said, "Home?" as if he'd read her mind. And Shannon jumped at the suggestion.

Shannon was grateful when they finally reached it that Dag's truck was already running again—thanks to his remote starter—so he could instantly push the heat to full blast. Then he left her there to warm up while he ran into the Groceries and Sundries without telling her why.

"The fixings for my famous hot chocolate!" he announced when he returned to the truck and got in, holding a bag in the air as if it were a prize of war. "I'll build you a fire, fix you a cup of that and you'll forget all about being frozen."

"Who says I'm frozen?" Shannon said defensively.

"Not who, what—those two bright red cheeks and that even brighter red nose." He flipped down the visor on the passenger side and pointed to the mirror there. "See for yourself, Rudolph," he teased as he put the truck into gear and pulled away from the curb. "There I was, skating along, looking at where we were going instead of at you, and then I catch a glimpse of your face and you're all lit up!"

Shannon didn't know whether to laugh or cry at the way she looked, but she *was* a sight—her nose and cheeks were beet-red.

Before she'd reacted in any way, Dag said, "Why didn't you tell me that you were cold?"

"And let you think I'm a sissy?" she challenged. "Besides, I shouldn't have been any colder than you."

"*Ice* hockey, remember? I'm used to it. Apparently they heat kindergarten rooms, huh?" he added with a wry glance in her direction.

Shannon just laughed, glad that they'd reached the garage apartment.

While Dag built a fire, Shannon went to do some damage control. First—following his orders—she removed the socks she had on and replaced them with two pairs of dry, heavier ones she'd snatched from a drawer and brought into the studio apartment's bathroom with her. After that she focused on what she was most concerned with and went to the mirror above the sink.

She was glad to discover that her nose was no longer bright red and that her cheeks had calmed to merely a rosy glow. The knit cap she'd worn and now removed had mussed her hair, so she put a brush through it and then applied a little lip gloss.

Despite the calming of her coloring, she was still feeling chilled when she left the bathroom, so she made a beeline for the fireplace.

"Fire is definitely more my speed than ice," she said with one last shiver.

"You *are* a sissy," he teased, bringing two steaming cups with him when he joined her.

Shannon took one of the mugs he offered, first encircling it with both hands to warm them and then tasting the rich, frothy brew that it held. "Oh, wow, you and chocolate must be a match made in heaven—this is *not* everyday stuff."

"It's my special blend," he said, not offering exactly what that special blend was.

But all Shannon cared about was chasing away the chill and enjoying her hot chocolate, and to that end she sat on the hearth and sipped.

Dag sat beside her, leaving a few inches between them. Not too many inches, but enough so that there was no touching—except in Shannon's mind where she was imagining his thigh running the length of her thigh, and his upper body close enough for her to snuggle against....

Trying to ignore that image, she glanced sideways

at his oh-so-handsome, slightly beard-shadowed face with its rugged appeal, and said, "Professional hockey, huh?"

"Guilty."

"Playing professional sports of any kind is the dream of a lot of little boys."

"Playing pro-hockey was mine, that's for sure. It was already something I was fantasizing about and acting out with my friends when I asked for my first pair of skates."

"Which was when?" Shannon probed to learn more about him.

"I was four. There was a pond near our house that froze solid every winter. All the kids skated there and the bigger guys played hockey. I was itching to get in on the action. So I asked for the skates for Christmas and the minute I put them on they just felt right. I knew I was going to be able to fly in them—"

"That seems so young," Shannon marveled.

Dag laughed. "I know guys who think if their kid can walk, he can skate, to get a head start in the game."

"And you were a natural?"

"Let's just say I was a quick learner. But I was right about the skates—once I learned how to get around on them, I could move as if my feet had wings."

"And because of the older guys playing hockey, rather than figure skating, you went in that direction?" Shannon asked after another sip of her hot chocolate.

"I didn't even know what figure skating was as a kid. But hockey was everywhere around here. I played in the amateur league, I spent two summers in Canada at hockey camp, and I played one season of midget before I finally started high school and could play there—"

"And then through college," she contributed, recalling that he'd said he'd had a scholarship, "before you went pro."

"Right," he confirmed, drinking his own hot chocolate quicker than she was.

"You must have been really good."

"Good enough," he said.

But this evening someone had marveled at Dag being twice-named MVP, so she knew he was being humble.

"Was it all you'd hoped it would be?" she asked, wondering why he wasn't still doing it.

"Oh, God, yes," he answered heartily. "Making a living doing something you love? Being treated like a king by fans? By women—"

Shannon laughed at that. "Groupies?"

"Some…" he said the same way he'd refrained from bragging about his skills. But rather than elaborating on that, he went on talking about how hockey had been everything he'd hoped it would be.

"But it doesn't make for a long career?" she said to encourage him to tell her why he wasn't still playing.

Dag shrugged. "Some guys make it into their forties. One guy played until he was fifty-two."

"But you…"

"I'm definitely not forty or fifty-two," he said wryly.

"But you're not still playing the game you love," she persisted.

"Nope, now I'm a land- and homeowner," he said.

Shannon sensed that his positive attitude about this change was some sort of spin, that he wasn't actually happy to have stopped playing hockey.

And her feeling grew stronger when he abruptly changed the subject. "So, your face is back to its normal color. How about your hands and feet—any pain? Can you feel all of your fingers and toes?"

"I'm fine."

"I can stop worrying about frostbite and hypothermia?"

Shannon smiled. "*Were* you worrying about me having frostbite and hypothermia?"

"A little," he admitted.

She knew it shouldn't matter, but it felt good that he'd been concerned, that he cared. Not that it meant anything, she told herself in order to keep from reading more into it than she should.

She did, however, sorely regret it when Dag stood then and said, "I should probably get going."

She wanted to say, *Do you have to?*

But she didn't. She just stood, too, and walked him to the door.

"I can't thank you enough for today…and tonight—"

"Don't thank me at all," he said as they reached the door and he was shrugging into his coat. "I got my own Christmas shopping finished, too."

But once his coat was in place, he turned to face her and added in a quieter tone, "Besides, I had a great time. Getting into town, having pizza, an hour on the ice, hot chocolate in front of a fire—all of it with you—there's no chore in any of that." Then he smiled a slow, sexy smile. "Actually, now that I think about it, maybe *I* should be thanking *you*."

Even knowing nothing about hockey or its players, Shannon connected the sport with bruisers, not with charmers. But as she smiled up at Dag, it was his charm that was getting to her.

And his dark eyes.

And his chiseled features.

And everything else about him…

And it all suddenly bowled her over and left her unable to recall another time, another man, she'd ever wanted to have kiss her quite as much as she wanted that man to kiss her at that moment.

It was so potent tonight that it seemed impossible to hide what was on her mind and she felt her chin tip upward with a will of its own, silently sending a message.

Dag smiled a small, knowing smile and grasped her upper arm, sliding down to catch her hand, to enclose it in his and hold it tight.

Don't just hold my hand…and please don't just kiss that again tonight…

But that's what he did.

And despite the fact that the kiss lingered longer than it had the night before, despite the fact that his thumb did a sexy massage on the top of her wrist, Shannon couldn't help wishing that chivalry was dead and buried!

But he thinks you're engaged, a little voice in the back of her head reminded her.

And she'd given her word that she wouldn't tell anyone otherwise.…

Then Dag squeezed her hand and lingered at that, too, as if he were having trouble giving her up.

And no matter how much Shannon willed him not to, he still did, saying, "G'night," in a tone that seemed to shout, *If only things were different…*

And it was so tempting to tell him that they were!

But she didn't. She merely whispered back, "Good night," trying to keep the disappointment from her voice as she watched him flip up the collar on his coat and slip outside into snow that had begun to fall since they'd arrived home.

Then she closed the door and pressed her forehead to it, sighing a deep sigh of regret.

But Dag was right in practicing restraint, she told herself. Right to be respectful of her supposed engagement.

And she was wrong, wrong, wrong to want him not to.

It was just that wrong, wrong, wrong or not, she still couldn't help wishing that he *would* have kissed her until she begged not to be kissed any more.

On the mouth!

Chapter Seven

A blizzard struck overnight and Shannon woke up Monday morning to a winter wonderland. And to two and a half feet of snow separating the garage apartment, Chase's loft and the main house.

The snow was still falling in big, fluffy potato-chip-size flakes as Chase shoveled a path between the loft and the garage, and Dag shoveled one from the rear entrance of the main house to the garage. By lunchtime the two connecting paths provided a way for Chase, Hadley, Cody and Shannon to join Meg, Logan, Tia and Dag for a snow day all together in the big farmhouse.

The Christmas lights were lit and Logan made sure the fire never got too low in the fireplace. They spent the early part of the afternoon munching on an abundance of fresh popcorn and drinking mulled cider while watching a Christmas movie.

When it was time for the kids to take naps, Chase

and Logan were dispatched to bed them down while Shannon, Hadley and Meg began cooking a roast for dinner, started dough to rise for homemade bread and made an apple pie that would go into the oven when the roast came out.

Then Meg and Hadley joined their mates for naps, too—Meg and Logan on the sofa, and Chase and Hadley in the overstuffed recliner—leaving Shannon and Dag on their own.

That was when Dag said to Shannon, "Why don't we go through the boxes of your grandmother's things from the house and find those pictures of you as a kid? We can do it in the kitchen without disturbing anybody and then you'll have them to start the photo albums."

Shannon jumped at the idea and while she cleared space on the big, country-kitchen table, Dag put on his fleece-lined suede coat.

He had to reshovel the path to the garage where her car was parked to get to it. Shannon watched from the window over the sink, enjoying the sight of the burly man cutting a swath through the pristine white powder. She was looking forward to a little time alone with him. More than she should be, she knew, but it didn't matter.

Should I tell him now or wait? she wondered as she watched.

She'd had a phone call from Wes's secretary before she'd even gotten out of bed this morning telling her to watch the evening news. The press had been invited to the Rumson compound for the arrival of all the Rumsons for their Christmas holiday. The secretary hadn't said that Wes would be announcing that the engagement was off, but Shannon couldn't think of any other reason why she would be encouraged to watch.

And if Wes was finally going to go public with the

news, then it didn't seem like it would do any harm for her to tell Dag only a few hours earlier, when they were snowbound and it wasn't likely for her secret to get beyond the walls of the house.

Except that again she thought of the vow she'd made not to tell anyone, and decided she could probably wait those few hours herself.

But she was definitely going to be glad when she didn't have to continue this charade.

The frustration of wanting Dag to kiss her good-night the last few evenings and not having it happen came to mind just then, accompanied by the fleeting idea that this could change once he knew she was free.

She pushed those thoughts away and reminded herself that the illusion of an engagement was not the only reason she shouldn't be kissing Dag McKendrick, that her life was in flux, that her time with him was just a brief interlude, and that she couldn't allow herself to be swept up in the cozy comfort she was experiencing here, with him.

But a tiny, secret part of her, deep down inside, was still excited at the prospect of finally having it known that she wasn't engaged to Wes Rumson. And seeing what happened...

"I didn't bring the box with the blankets and clothes in it," Dag said when he returned to the warmth of the kitchen with only one of the two cardboard boxes he'd filled for her at her grandmother's house. "The pictures should be in this one—I put them in the jewelry box so they wouldn't get any more worn than they already are."

Shannon rummaged through the box of odds and ends until she found an old jewelry box she remembered playing with as a child—it was cream colored with an inlay of flowers on top, and when the lid was lifted, a tiny ballerina sprang up from the center of the top tier of velvet-lined compartments.

"I loved this as a kid," she told Dag. "When you wind it up—" which she did, using the turnkey hidden on the back "—it plays music and the ballerina dances."

Surprisingly, it still worked, and for a moment Shannon watched the ballerina turn on her pedestal just like she had as a child.

Then the music ran out, the ballerina came to a stop, and Dag said, "The pictures are in the bottom. Oh, and there's a ring, too—that was in the jewelry box when I found it. I forgot about that until just now."

Shannon retrieved the ring first, remembering it, too. "This was my grandmother's—she got it when she turned sixteen," she explained of the delicate gold band with three small amethyst stones set in it. "It only has sentimental value, but I'm glad it wasn't lost."

She slipped it on her left ring finger. "I used to pretend it was my wedding ring," she confided with a laugh, holding out her hand, fingers splayed upward the way she had done many times in her young life on visits to her grandmother.

"I suppose you could use it for that now, but I'm betting the wife of a Rumson is supposed to have something flashier."

Letting his remark pass, Shannon said, "I think I'll get a chain for it and wear it as a necklace, instead."

She took off the ring and set it in the top tier of the jewelry box beside the ballerina. Then she reached into the lower portion for the photographs she'd spotted there.

They were a little ragged from age and the wear and

tear of wherever they'd been hiding until Dag found them, but Shannon thought they were still usable.

She set them all out on the table.

"There's six," Dag said. "I thought there were five."

"Five of me," Shannon said, looking over four photographs of her taken the summer she was nine, all of them from a Fourth of July picnic she remembered. The fifth snapshot was from her last visit to Northbridge when she was not quite twelve—looking gangly and awkward.

"Oh, this one is bad!" she said with a laugh. "My mom gave me a perm just before I came here and it was sooo awful!"

Dag picked up that picture to take a closer look at it and laughed, too. "That *is* pretty bad. You look like you're wearing a fright wig."

"I don't think that one is going into albums."

"Ah, come on, Chase would get a kick out of it. Give him that one *and* one of the others—he should get two since it's his Christmas present."

"I'll have to think about that…" was the most Shannon would concede to.

Dag replaced the fright-wig photo on the table and studied the others.

"These are good, though," he decreed. "You just look like a happy kid."

"Probably because that's what I was."

"So that's something to share with the brothers who weren't there to know you then."

"What's this other one?" Shannon said as she picked up the sixth picture.

Sitting next to her at the oval table, he stretched an arm across the top of her high-backed chair to lean over and peer at the photograph, too.

He was wearing a plaid flannel shirt with a white

thermal T-shirt visible underneath it, and a pair of jeans. He had a fresh, woodsy smell to him that seemed warm and cozy, and between that and having his big body only inches away, something inside of Shannon went a little weak.

She made a conscious effort not to lean in even nearer to him, but it did take some forethought because she felt an almost magnetic pull toward him.

Just look at the picture, she told herself sternly, forcing herself to do that.

"It's Gramma," she said as she did. "And me, I think—that looks like me in the pictures my parents took when they first got me. I don't recognize that other woman, though, or those two really small babies she's holding…"

"I didn't look at these when I found them, but now that I am…if I'm not mistaken, that other woman is a young Liz Rudolph," Dag said. "Turn it over, I think there's something written on the back."

Shannon did as he'd suggested, reading what was there along with the date. *"Liz and me with the new members of our families."*

Shannon flipped the picture over again to study it even more closely. "It's the right year, the year I was adopted. And those babies are twins—they look just alike. Could this be a picture of my twin brothers?"

"The new members of our families," Dag repeated what was scribbled on the back of the photo. "You were the new member of Carol's family. The twins were what—two months old—when they were adopted?"

"Yes."

"I don't know much about babies but those are some pretty small ones. And you're right—they do look alike, so I'd guess they were twins, too. I'd say it's possible they're your brothers."

Shannon continued to stare at the photograph as if she might see something else in it if she looked long enough. "You know this Liz person?"

"Liz Rudolph. She's your grandmother's age. Of course my earliest memory of her is long after this. But maybe she and your grandmother were friends."

"Was she related to that couple Chase said adopted the twins—Lila and Tony Bruno?"

"I've never heard those names other than from Chase. The reverend told him that he placed the twins with the Brunos. But Liz could be related to the president and I wouldn't know it. I only know Liz because when I was a teenager I mowed her lawn a few summers after her husband died. It wasn't as if we talked or anything."

"Is she still living? And around here?"

"Actually, she moved out of town to be nearer to her sister after my third summer of mowing. But you're in luck because rather than sell her house, she rented it all this time and she moved back into it this summer—I met her at the post office about a week after I got here in September. We were both picking up forwarded mail."

"So Chase and I could talk to her…"

"She's a nice lady, I don't know why not. Chase may or may not remember her, but when the snow clears I can take you over there and introduce the two of you. We could bring the picture with us and ask her about it."

The old photograph was the topic of conversation all through dinner. Meg, Logan, Hadley and Chase all knew Liz Rudolph by name—as an older woman who had lived in Northbridge when they were all kids. But none of them knew anything more about her or were even aware that she'd returned to Northbridge.

Both Shannon and Chase were encouraged by the possibility that the infants in the picture could be their lost siblings, though, and that they might suddenly have a way of garnering some information about what had happened to them. But Shannon's general excitement over that and the pleasure she was finding in the day both ebbed slightly after the family had all watched the evening news at her prompting.

Wes's secretary was right—there was a report on Wes arriving with the rest of his extended family at the Rumson compound, which was decorated in Christmas splendor. But even when one reporter asked where Wes's fiancée was, he merely said Shannon was spending Christmas with her own family this year. No announcement was made that he did not actually have a fiancée.

Shannon was still steaming over that fact when she placed a call to Wes after dinner and left him the curt message to please call her back.

Of course he didn't do that immediately so she silently simmered all through the evening of board games.

Then the power went out and while both couples decided the best thing to do was just get the kids and themselves into nice warm beds for the night, Dag volunteered to go out to the garage apartment with Shannon, build a fire for her for heat, and set her up with candles and flashlights so she would be prepared should the power not be restored until morning.

It wasn't an offer Shannon could make herself refuse, and so she and Dag bundled up and she followed behind him as he reshoveled the path between mounting walls of snow to the garage apartment.

Dag had just lit two candles for light and begun to

put the logs in the fireplace when Wes finally returned Shannon's call.

"I have to take this," she told Dag when she checked to see who her caller was.

"Want me to make myself scarce and come back in a little while?"

A scarcity of Dag was the last thing she wanted, especially in a blackout, and she could not, in good conscience, make him leave and come back.

"No, it's okay," she said, moving across the small studio apartment to the kitchen section to talk with her back to Dag while he went on laying the fire.

"Wes," she said into the phone when she answered it, keeping her voice low even though she knew Dag probably still couldn't help overhearing it.

"Can you hold on just a minute?" was Wes Rumson's response.

He didn't wait for her to answer before she could hear him talking to his campaign manager—who also happened to be his cousin—about the photo opportunities that would be provided by Christmas shopping in Butte the following day.

Then Wes came back on the line. "Sorry. You know how it is."

Too well.

"How are you? Is everything all right?" Wes asked then.

"No, it isn't," Shannon said tightly to keep her voice from rising the way it was inclined to do. "When your secretary called this morning to tell me to watch the news tonight I thought it was because you were making the announcement."

"She didn't tell you that, did she?"

"No, it was what I assumed because it needs to be

done, you said you would do it and it should have been done long before now," Shannon said a bit heatedly.

Wes ignored that and said, "I was just thinking about how much you liked it here when you visited that one time—remember? It occurred to me that maybe if you saw the place again on TV and pictured yourself here with me next Christmas—the way you could be—you might change your mind."

So his secretary calling to make sure she watched the news had been a manipulation. Much like the trip they'd taken to Europe a few months earlier.

Shannon shook her head despite the fact that Wes couldn't see how much that irked her.

"I saw it all on the news," she said curtly. "It didn't change my mind. You *need* to make the announcement."

"Everywhere I go, every hand I shake, people want to know when the wedding is. Yesterday Bill Muny and I were both at the same event—"

Bill Muny was the gubernatorial candidate for the other party.

"—and every reporter flocked to me, all wanting to know about you and the wedding. Bill Muny couldn't get the time of day from any one of them! Plus it's Christmas, Shannon. No one wants to hear about breakups now."

"In other words, you aren't going to announce it until when?"

Silence.

"Wes…" Shannon said through clenched teeth. "You need to do this."

"When the time is right—you left it to me, remember? Are you going back on that?"

"It's getting more and more difficult for me," she said,

thinking of Dag, knowing he shouldn't be a factor and reasoning that she also didn't like having to pretend with Chase and Hadley and Logan and Meg, either. Or with any of the other people she was meeting in Northbridge now who all believed she was engaged.

"I just don't think it can be done before the holidays," Wes said then. "It could kill my momentum and I might not be able to pick up speed again. If we release the story in January, there could be some sympathy and that could carry us over."

"Sympathy? Are you going to make me the villain in this? I thought we agreed that you would say it was a mutual decision!"

Okay, that time her voice *had* gotten a little louder and she knew Dag must have heard. But she couldn't help it. She didn't want to have to face public scorn for rejecting one of Montana's favorite sons any more than she liked having to pretend she was engaged.

"Sure, yes, right—we'll say it was a mutual decision," Wes said insincerely.

"And that you didn't want to be distracted from your dedication to the constituents—that's what you said you would say so it sounded like you were doing it for the good of your voters," she reminded insistently because she'd thought that if he took that tack neither of them would come out the worse for wear.

"We can't have it sound as if I dumped you—no one votes for a heel," Wes countered.

"Which is why I agreed to make at least one public appearance with you after you make the announcement so everyone can see that there are no hard feelings."

"Still…"

Shannon knew at that moment that she was likely to come out of this looking like the bad guy. But at this point, she was even willing to accept that to have it over with.

"Just do it, Wes," she said definitively then. "Just do it!" she repeated before hanging up on him.

For a moment she remained where she was, leaning against the island counter, keeping her back to Dag, considering what to say to him.

After the phone call, she thought that he might well have guessed that the engagement was off. And if that was the case, then it seemed better to come clean so she could impress upon him the importance of keeping her secret.

Having made her decision, she turned around. Dag was adjusting the fireplace screen, his suede coat still on.

"You could take off your coat and stay awhile…" she said softly, removing her own coat now that the fire was roaring and providing enough heat so that she didn't need more than the jeans and heavy cable-knit sweater she was wearing.

"Okay," he agreed without the need for more persuasion.

He removed his coat, too, tossing it on the sofa where Shannon had placed hers. Then they each sat on a bar stool at the island counter, sitting at angles to face each other.

"I'm sure you heard some of that call," Shannon said then, opting to cut to the chase.

"I tried not to listen," he said with a smile full of mischief. "But this *is* a pretty small place…"

"If I tell you the truth, you have to make a solemn promise that it stays just between you and me."

"Things are not what they appear with you and the potential future-Governor," Dag guessed.

"You have to make a solemn promise," Shannon repeated.

"Cross my heart," he joked, using a long index finger to draw an *X* over one side of that impressively massive chest of his.

"I'm not joking," Shannon said when she'd forced herself not to feast her eyes for too long on that portion of his body and looked at his ruggedly gorgeous face again. "I gave my word that this wouldn't get out until Wes's public relations people have found exactly the right time, exactly the right spin to put on it."

"And you think I might rush out of here, put in a call to the newspapers and news stations, and tell them whatever you tell me? Come on," he cajoled. "I wouldn't do that to you."

She was aware that she barely knew this man, and yet she somehow did believe that he wouldn't do anything to bring harm to her.

"Okay, I'm trusting you…" she said anyway before she confided, "I'm not engaged to Wes Rumson."

Dag grinned a grin so big it was clear he wasn't sorry to hear that. And he didn't pretend to be. But he did say, "So explain, because I saw it myself—nobody could have missed it since the news stations played it over and over again. First Rumson announced he was running for governor, then he took you by the hand to stand next to him at the microphone and said if you'd have him, he wanted to introduce you as the future Mrs. Wesley Rumson."

Shannon remembered the moment vividly. The crowd of Wes's supporters and the bevy of reporters had cheered, Wes had raised her hand into the air as a gesture of victory, and what else could she do but smile even as panic had rushed through her?

And of course the assumption had been that she was accepting his proposal…

"I know it looked as if I said yes," she said. "But if you'll recall, I didn't say anything at all. In fact, I had already made up my mind to break things off with Wes before that. I just hadn't found a minute alone with him to do it—which was part of why I *wouldn't* marry him."

"Take me back to square one—how did you get together with Wes Rumson in the first place?"

"Three years ago my friend Dani and her husband treated me to a ski trip to Aspen for New Year's. Dani's husband is…well, he's rich, so everything we did—where we stayed, where we skied, where we ate—was top-of-the-line, among a whole lot of bigwigs. Wes and his cousin were some of those bigwigs. Wes noticed that I was the third wheel with Dani and her husband, and since he was the third wheel with his cousin and his cousin's wife—"

"You formed your own couple?"

"It actually started as a running joke, something he used to flirt with me. Then he asked me for a drink. We started staying in the bar after the couples went up to their rooms for the night. We were both from Montana, so we had that in common. He lives primarily in Billings, I live in Billings. He asked if I'd go out with him once we were both home again, and I…" Shannon shrugged. "I did say yes to that."

"And it went from there."

"Wes called soon after we were both in Billings again, and yes, it went from there. We started dating and eventually we were serious enough to talk marriage."

"But…"

"Dating a Rumson is not like dating someone else.

Wes is the Rumson family's hope for the future in politics. He's the center of their political machine. *That's* his priority and the priority of everyone around him—his personal life doesn't really exist. His personal life is more a tool used to make him look good to voters, it isn't something he actually indulges in much."

"No seeing more and more of each other until you became an inseparable couple?"

"Dating Wes meant we saw each other when it worked out—and that definitely didn't make us inseparable. But until about six months ago, that was okay with me. I liked Wes. I grew to care about him—I still care about him. He's a decent man. But I was swamped myself. I was working and taking care of my parents, so I didn't really have any more time for Wes than he had for me."

"Until six months ago," Dag repeated what she'd said.

"Actually, I began to have doubts about the relationship when my Dad died. I would have liked to have had Wes be there for me more than he was."

"But he wasn't?"

"He made it to the funeral, he sent flowers and condolences, he had his secretary check with me every day for a while, but no. Things were the same with him—he was busy. And it really hit home for me then that I wasn't his top priority, even when there was a reason I should be."

"But you didn't break it off with him then?"

Shannon shrugged again. "I still had Mom to take care of and Gramma was with us, so I didn't make a big deal out of it, but I did start considering whether or not I wanted to go through life never being who or what came first with Wes."

"Then your mom passed away—did he step up any better for that?"

Shannon shook her head. "It was about the same and then out of the blue, Gramma died..."

"Which was a shock," Dag recalled.

She didn't know why it touched her that he remembered how difficult it had been. But it did touch her and suddenly tears threatened. She looked at the fire for a moment to blink them away before she brought her gaze back to his chiseled features.

"I just couldn't believe I'd lost Gramma, too," she confirmed. "And I really didn't know where to turn, so Wes was the first person I called. But I got his cousin—"

"The campaign manager?"

"Right—Mose Rumson. Mose said Wes was having a drink with an important contributor and I couldn't talk to him. I said it was an emergency, that my grandmother had had a heart attack. Mose still wouldn't put Wes on, he said he'd have him call me back, and Wes didn't even do that until the next day—"

"You have to be kidding me?"

"Mose held off telling him, so it wasn't really Wes's fault—"

"Still! Did he deck that guy when he found out?"

Shannon shook her head. "Wes made excuses for him."

"He took the cousin's side?" Dag said, sounding outraged on her behalf.

"Basically. And when it came to the funeral I thought—I was hoping—that since I really was alone for that one, Wes would do more—"

"But he didn't."

"He sent his mother. And she was great, she stayed with me, she went through all the arrangements with me,

I couldn't have done it without her. But no, Wes came to the funeral, he paid for a catered luncheon after the burial, but he didn't show up for it, and after spending so much time with his mother and talking to her about her own marriage and how this was life as the wife of a Rumson, I was just about done."

"*Just about,* but *still* not completely?"

"I was so...*alone* then," she said. "And Wes was always apologetic about how little we saw each other, about his distractions and all the interference. When Gramma died and he didn't do more, he promised to make it up to me with a month in Europe. Just the two of us. I thought there might be some hope for us...I guess I was *hoping* there might be some hope for us."

"I heard that Chase tried to get hold of you but couldn't for a long time because you were in Europe, so Rumson must have come through on the trip?"

"He did. We did go to Europe. But not by ourselves. We went with Mose and his wife, and it ended up being Wes and Mose working on the campaign while Mose's wife was dispatched to take me sightseeing. And that was when I'd really had it," Shannon said conclusively. "I wanted—want—a bigger life, and being the woman-behind-Wes, being Mrs. Wes Rumson, could have been that. But I also want the kind of relationship my parents had with each other and I knew then that that would never be what I had with Wes."

"Plus, maybe I'm wrong," Dag ventured, "but it doesn't sound like you had the kind of feelings for him that your parents had for each other, either."

Shannon couldn't deny that. "I kept thinking that might come with time, but no, I finally admitted that to myself, too."

"So you were going to end it with him," Dag prompted.

"But again, once we got back, I kept trying to get a minute with him and never could. I didn't want to break up over the phone, but I *had* told him that I needed to see him alone, that we needed to talk—which seemed like it should have been a clue as to what I was going to do—"

"It would have been to me," Dag agreed.

"But Wes couldn't fit me in before the announcement that he was running for governor. He said he wanted me there with him for that and I said I would come, but only if he swore that afterward we could talk. The next thing I knew, I was by his side in front of all those people and there was that public proposal and the assumption that of course I would marry him. The minute we were behind closed doors after that I told him I wouldn't. That cleared the room, let me tell you…"

Dag laughed. "I'll bet."

"So there never actually was an engagement," Shannon concluded.

"But that was almost a month ago and—"

"I know! Since it *looked* as if I'd said yes, it became a big deal how it was presented that we *aren't* getting married. I agreed to let Wes's public relations people handle making that announcement in a way that won't damage Wes's run for governor. But it keeps not happening! When his secretary called to tell me to watch the news tonight, I thought for sure it was because they were finally going to say it—"

"But they didn't…"

Why had Dag's tone turned so ominous when he said that?

"Is that because Rumson is hanging on, hoping you'll change your mind?" Dag asked.

"There's a little of that," Shannon admitted.

"Maybe he has deeper feelings for you than you think."

"It isn't that I don't think Wes has feelings for me. But I don't believe that's what's really causing the delay. He keeps talking about how much attention the engagement is getting his campaign. He doesn't want to lose that more than he doesn't want to lose me. And he certainly doesn't want to lose any of the votes that a wedding might have gotten him."

Dag didn't say anything to that, he just looked slightly skeptical.

"But the bottom line is that I am *not* engaged to Wes Rumson," Shannon said firmly. "You just can't tell anyone."

"Chase and Logan and Hadley and Meg would keep the secret," Dag said then.

"I know they probably would, but I said I wouldn't say anything until Wes's people handled it the best way possible and I'm trying to stick to that…"

"Well, I won't tell anyone. But if you decide to, you could. Without worrying about it."

The power came on then—light from outside could suddenly be seen through the windows and the sound of the refrigerator running again alerted them to it.

Dag got up and turned on the lamp beside the sofa. "Looks like we're back in business," he said.

But it was so nice sitting here in the fire glow—come back…

Apparently he couldn't hear her thoughts because rather than rejoining her, Dag snatched his coat from the couch and said, "And it's late so I should let you get to bed and turn in myself—if I get an early start shoveling us out tomorrow, we might be able to make it to see Liz Rudolph in the afternoon."

Disappointed, Shannon stood up to walk him to the door.

It was there that he put his coat on, leaving it unbuttoned but jamming his hands into the pockets.

And out of the blue Shannon wanted to snake her hands inside the fleece-lined suede and snuggle between its open ends, up against that broad chest...

She chased away the urge and the image, and glanced up at Dag's face. But that didn't help much since the man was so heart-stoppingly handsome and he was standing so close in front of her, peering down at her with those piercing black eyes.

"*Not* engaged, huh?" he said in a voice that was quiet and deeper than it had been.

"*Not* engaged. Not now. Not ever. Never have been."

"That changes things, doesn't it?" he mused. "That means you're a free agent..."

"I guess I am," she said.

"And *I* am..."

"Are you? We haven't really talked about that..."

"Oh, I am! Believe me, I am!"

His enthusiasm made her curious. But all she did was smile because quizzing him on his romantic past wasn't what she was really interested in doing at that moment. Not when, once again, thoughts of kissing him were tiptoeing around the edges of her mind. And hope had a new hold on her...

Then Dag took one hand from his coat pocket and raised it to the side of her face. Her cheek, her jaw, fit into the sturdy palm he laid there.

He went on looking into her eyes and even though he still wasn't kissing her, she was at least glad that he hadn't gone for a peck on her hand again.

Then he used a gentle pressure to tip her head slightly back. He came forward, and after what seemed like an eternity of hovering a scant inch from his target, he pressed his mouth to hers.

She couldn't help the tiny sigh that escaped when that finally happened. But if Dag noticed it, it didn't make any difference because he merely went on kissing her.

His lips were tender and adept and parted just slightly. His breath was warm. And there was a sweet sway to his head that Shannon was caught up in as she answered every bit of that kiss, letting it—helping it—grow and deepen and go on long enough for her to savor it and wish with all her might that it would go on and on...

For a little while it did just that. It went on as if Dag didn't want it to end any more than she did. But eventually it had to, and when it did Shannon found herself light-headed.

"Not engaged," Dag repeated in a husky voice for her ears alone.

"Not engaged," Shannon echoed.

Then he opened the door and went out into the cold winter night, calling over his shoulder, "I'll see you tomorrow," and disappearing down the stairs.

But Shannon ignored the chilly air and craned her head out the door so she could watch him go, still feeling the heat he'd left behind on her lips, in her blood.

And thinking that that kiss had just added one more thing that Wes couldn't compare to.

Chapter Eight

As Dag shoveled snow the next day, his mind was in turmoil and not even the quiet of the winter countryside or the rhythmic repetition of the work could stop it.

So Shannon was not engaged, he kept thinking.

But she still wanted a bigger life.

She wasn't engaged.

But she still had Wes Rumson hot on her trail.

She wasn't engaged.

But even if she stuck to her guns about Rumson, she was probably headed for a bigger life with that school in Beverly Hills.

So if anything, he should give her a wider berth now than he had before, he told himself. Because before, he was just struggling with his attraction to someone who was engaged to someone else and completely off-limits to him. But now?

Now what made her off-limits to him was less

concrete. No less valid. But a whole lot more wobbly a barrier to protect him from himself and his own inclinations when it came to Shannon.

Inclinations like the one to kiss her.

He'd managed to control that when he'd believed she was engaged to another guy. But last night? Last night he'd kissed her. And wanted to kiss her again and again and again...

Jeez, he thought he'd learned his lesson about staying away from a woman who had another man on the hook in any way. He thought he knew, inside and out, to avoid women who weren't satisfied with who they were or what they had.

But maybe he didn't know anything, maybe he hadn't learned anything, because what was he doing now?

He was panting after a woman who had her sights set on greater things than a small ranch in a small town— whether it was being a politician's wife or owning a school in Beverly Hills. A woman who might be saying that her relationship with Wes Rumson was over, but who was still having contact with him, still admitting that she cared for him, still not *completely* finished with him.

Dag just didn't seem to be able to stop himself.

Yes, she was beautiful and maybe if that was all there was to it, it would be easier to maintain some control. But he also liked her. A lot. She was nice, she was kind, she was calm, she was good with the kids, she was funny and easy to talk to. She wasn't judgmental, she was sexier than she seemed to know, and more down-to-earth than she might want to be. And every minute he was with her was so good he didn't want it to end.

But it was going to end! One way or another, when Christmas was over, Shannon Duffy was gone.

And if he was in too deep with her, it was going to be his own tough luck, he told himself when he'd finished the path from the front porch out to the drive that ran along the house.

But as he turned the corner to shovel from the side of the house to the garage—where Logan was starting an old tractor he and Chase had bought with a blade attached to the front of it to deal with the driveway snow removal—Dag's perspective suddenly took a turn, too.

Wasn't he getting ahead of himself when it came to Shannon? Wasn't he thinking about things on too large a scale?

There wasn't actually much time at stake. Christmas was in a few days. How deep could he get in just a few days? Especially knowing that that was all the time he was going to have with her? Why was he thinking about her in an all-or-nothing way?

Traveling for hockey—to training camp, to tournaments, on publicity tours—there had been plenty of times when he'd known he was only going to be in a city for a short time. But if he'd met someone he was interested in, attracted to, that hadn't kept him from asking them out.

Brief was better than nothing, and that hadn't meant a string of one-night stands. Sure there had been those, too. But sometimes nothing had come of things but a dinner or two, some clubbing, maybe an afternoon at a museum or a zoo. Just some relaxation, some fun, some entertainment, some company. Why was he thinking this thing with Shannon was any different?

Sure, after the fiasco with Sandra, after the end of hockey, after settling in Northbridge again, he'd been doing more thinking about settling down with one particular woman. But who said Shannon was that one particular woman? Or that he couldn't have this time with her the way he'd had short-lived times with other women—knowing it would come to an end—before he moved on to looking for that one particular woman?

It was no big deal. He would just do what he'd done on those other occasions—go with the flow. He'd done it in the past, why couldn't he do that now?

Shannon *wasn't* engaged so it wouldn't be cheating on her part, or anything sleazy on his. True, he had vowed to steer clear of any situation that even resembled his last one. But the last relationship had gotten serious. And this one wouldn't. So that made it different.

And it was Shannon who was moving on after Christmas, Shannon who would be leaving him behind. If she was willing to see him before that, to let him kiss her, why was he sweating it?

Just don't take it for anything more than it is, he advised himself.

And he thought he could do that. That he could be okay with a casual holiday hook up—if it went that far. He could be okay with going with the flow as long as he kept in mind that things with Shannon would end.

And he would definitely keep that in mind, he decided. But in the meantime he could have a few days, he could have Christmas, with Shannon.

Then she'd go her way, he'd go his.

And as for kissing her?

He knew he was likely to do that again because he couldn't even stop thinking about it.

As long as he didn't lose sight of the fact that there was an end to whatever it was that was between them, it would keep him from getting too attached and he could just enjoy the ride and be happy for whatever time he got with her and however far it went.

But the end *would* come, he reminded himself.

Time with Shannon was like Christmas cookies—they were around now, he enjoyed them, indulged in them, but when Christmas was over, that was it for the treats.

And after Christmas was over this year, that would be it for his time with Shannon, too.

But at least he'd have had this time with her, and in the same way he wouldn't deny himself the cookies just because they weren't around forever, he couldn't deny himself these few days with her, either...

It was midafternoon before the snow-shoveling was complete, before Dag and Chase decided they could probably make it into Northbridge to visit Liz Rudolph.

Shannon was curious about what had happened to her other brothers and eager to get any information. But Monday's snow day had been so nice she wouldn't have minded putting off the visit until Wednesday and having a second snow day today.

Or was it just a second day secluded with Dag that she wouldn't have minded having? she wondered as she sat close beside him on the bench seat of his truck with Chase on the passenger's side.

She decided that it might be wiser not to delve too deeply into that possibility, but she certainly didn't have any complaints about the tight quarters that had her sitting right up next to Dag as he drove.

Unfortunately when he was forced to plow the truck through a mound of snow to get onto Liz Rudolph's driveway, sitting so snugly next to him caused Shannon's shoulder to jab into Dag's rib cage.

"Sorry," she said.

Dag grinned down at her. "For what, that tiny body-check? I've taken a little worse," he joked as he turned off the engine.

A well-dressed elderly woman was standing in the open doorway by the time the threesome maneuvered the narrow path of cleared cement to get up to the house. Petite, she stood straight and unbowed by time. Her silver hair was in a perfect bob around her lined face and she looked very much just like an older version of the woman in the picture—unlike Shannon's grandmother who had gathered many pounds over the years and had not aged quite so gracefully.

Liz Rudolph greeted Dag warmly as she ushered them inside and closed the door behind them.

"I don't know if you remember Chase—" Dag said as they all accepted her invitation to take off their coats.

"I do. While I still lived here I was curious to watch you grow, knowing you were the twins' brother," she said as she draped each coat over a branch of a hall tree. "I was always praying that a nice family would take you but... Well, Alma Pritick was good to you as a foster mother, wasn't she?"

"She was," Chase assured.

Shannon noted that there was no mention of Chase's foster father, Homer, who Shannon knew hadn't abused Chase but had also not been a loving caregiver by any stretch of the imagination.

Then Liz Rudolph turned her attention to Shannon. "And you're Shannon," she said affectionately. "I was so, so sorry to hear about your mother and father. And then Carol...she and I were close all the years we both lived in Northbridge, and kept up with each other through Christmas cards when I moved away. I wanted to go to her funeral but I'd just had a pacemaker put in when I heard and I couldn't travel. I can't tell you how surprised and sorry I was..."

"It was very sudden and unexpected—it took me by surprise, too," Shannon said.

The older woman offered tea but when they all declined, she led them into her spotless living room where Shannon, Dag and Chase sat on the sofa facing the overstuffed chair Liz took. That was when Chase got to the point, showing her the photograph Shannon had found.

"We wondered if the babies in the picture are our brothers," he said.

"They are," the elderly woman answered without hesitation.

She repeated what they already knew about how they'd come to be in need of new homes.

"My sister's son and his wife wanted children and couldn't have them," she went on from there. "As tragic as the whole situation was—a young couple losing their lives, children orphaned—to Lila and Tony it was...well, it was a blessing. They were willing to take the twins so the twins wouldn't be separated from each other at least, and that went a long way in persuading Human Services to allow them to adopt the boys. And of course, Shannon, your mom and dad took you."

"Do you know why they—or Gramma—never told me there were other kids?" Shannon asked a question that had been on her mind since Chase had first contacted her.

"Oh, everyone just wanted to make their own little family. They didn't want it all spread out. Your grandmother and I were so close and we imagined that everyone might become one big happy family, but we were naive. Your parents wanted you to just be their little girl, without outside ties to anyone else. And Lila and Tony felt that way, too. Maybe it was sort of selfish, but in a way I understood—sometimes I think there's some insecurity connected to adoptions. Getting the twins away from here was actually part of why Lila and Tony left town when the babies were just six months old—they wanted to be somewhere where no one knew the twins as anything but their sons."

The older woman cast a guilty-looking glance at Chase and said, "Plus everyone felt bad about you, Chase. No one thought they could take on more, but being in the same small town with you, knowing you were at the boys' home all alone…"

Shannon saw Chase nod his understanding. But that seemed to be as much as Liz Rudolph wanted to say about the touchy subject because then she went right back to speaking mainly to Shannon as if they had more of a connection than she had with Chase.

"And then Lila and Tony's little family didn't even stay together," Liz informed her.

"They didn't?" Shannon asked.

The silver head shook. Liz pursed her lips disapprovingly for a moment before she said, "A year after Lila and Tony left, they divorced. Lila got custody of the twins and when my sister died, I lost contact with my nephew—"

"So, are you saying that you don't know what happened to the twins?" Shannon asked.

"I do know that by then my nephew Tony had been persuaded to give up his rights to the boys—they were barely two years old. But Lila had found a new husband and her new husband wanted to officially be their father since he'd be raising them. Tony was a housepainter and what he could provide for them just couldn't compare, so for their sake, he relinquished his paternity."

"What do you mean that what he could provide couldn't compare?" Chase asked.

"Lila married Morgan Kincaid," Liz Rudolph said with some awe in her voice.

"Morgan Kincaid the football player?" Shannon said to verify because while she didn't follow sports of any kind, Morgan Kincaid—and what he'd parlayed his football fame and fortune into—was well known in Montana.

"Morgan Kincaid," the elderly woman confirmed, "the football player, the owner of The Kincaid Corporation and all those restaurants and buildings and hotels and car dealerships and who knows what else," the elderly woman confirmed. "Those boys—Ian and Hutch they were called—ended up Kincaids."

Chapter Nine

"Why don't you guys go and I'll stay with the kids?" Shannon offered as dinner ended on Tuesday evening.

The plans for the night had been for them to drive into Northbridge for the Christmas Bazaar being held at the town square. But when Dag, Shannon and Chase had returned home from visiting Liz Rudolph that afternoon, both Tia and Cody seemed to be a little under the weather. After discussing that fact over another communal meal, the two couples decided that the kids shouldn't be taken out into the cold. That prompted Shannon to volunteer babysitting services so everyone else could go anyway.

"To tell you the truth, I think we all actually want to stay in tonight, don't we?" Meg insisted, looking around the rest of the group for support.

Hadley and Chase assured Shannon that they would rather watch TV tonight. Logan said he'd had enough of the snow for today and wanted nothing but to sit in front of a fire.

"I don't know," Dag piped up then. "It still sounds good to me. If it still sounds good to you, Shannon, why don't you and I go?"

And much to Shannon's dismay, *that* had more appeal than any of the other options.

So when the rest of the group chimed in with their encouragements, Shannon took up Dag on his counter-offer and the next thing she knew, she was in his truck again, headed for Northbridge and looking forward to seeing what else the small town did for the holiday.

And to once more spending the evening with Dag...

"So...proposed to by a Rumson, now related to Kincaids—maybe you not only *want* a bigger life, maybe you're destined to have one," Dag said as they turned from the driveway onto the road leading to Northbridge for the second time today. "How does it feel to be related to the Kincaid dynasty?"

Shannon laughed. "It feels exactly the same as it felt *not* being related to anyone in the *Kincaid dynasty*."

"What did you and Chase decide about contacting the twins after I dropped you off this afternoon?"

"We're trying to locate them," Shannon said. "We looked them up on the internet—there's a lot about Morgan Kincaid and The Kincaid Corporation, but less on Ian Kincaid or Hutch Kincaid. It looks like Ian works with something called an expansion football team..."

"Morgan Kincaid is bringing a pro-football team to Montana—it's been in all the papers and on the news. You must have heard about that..."

"I told you, I honestly don't pay any attention to

sports," Shannon said. "It could have been on the front page of the newspaper—"

"It has been—more than once."

"Even then, if it had to do with sports, I would have just turned to page two."

Dag laughed in disbelief and glanced at her. "I mean, it may not be hockey…" he said facetiously, "but football is pretty big, too. There's that whole Super Bowl thing and all."

"Still, I know nothing about sports and don't keep up with anything about them," Shannon said.

"Well, it's a big deal to get a new NFL franchise—a *huge* deal," he said, dumbfounded by how lightly she was taking that fact.

But all Shannon could do was shrug and say, "Okay."

Dag laughed again and shook his head in dismay. Then he went on with what Shannon actually did have an interest in. "But Ian Kincaid's name shows up in connection with the football team?"

"Right, he's listed on the website as the Chief Operating Officer so I guess that means he's on the business end of things. But we couldn't find anything recent on Hutch Kincaid at all. Apparently he played a lot of football himself a while ago, and was a star quarterback, but there's nothing current about him and he doesn't show up working for The Kincaid Corporation anywhere, so we're thinking the only way to reach him will be through Ian."

"But it sounds like you might be able to reach Ian."

"I hope so," Shannon said. "But sometimes the more public people are, the harder it is to get through to them."

"Like Wes Rumson, who can't even be reached by people he should be close to."

"Let alone by strangers with a story about long-lost siblings that the twins were probably never told they had," Shannon said. "There wasn't a way to email Ian Kincaid through the new football team, so we sent one through The Kincaid Corporation—we used a *Contact Us* tab on that website. We'll just have to see if the email gets to him."

"And if he answers it even if it does."

"True. I can tell you from my own experience with Chase that this whole thing comes as a shock and it's hard to believe. And I'm nobody—"

"Hey!"

"You know what I mean. I'm a kindergarten teacher, nothing high profile—"

"You were connected to a Rumson," he reminded.

"But until the public proposal, no one knew my name—in the few pictures of Wes and me at some charity function or another, if I wasn't cut out of the shot when it was printed, I was never included in the caption. It wasn't me who anyone cared to know. But for high-profile people, someone coming out of the woodwork with a weird claim—"

"Yeah, even if you're not high-profile but just in the public eye, sometimes people *do* come out of the woodwork with some crazy claim to get to you," Dag said as if he'd had experience with that. "And you're right, if it was me, I would probably think it was a prank or scam or something."

"And from what Liz said, I doubt if the twins were ever told anything about us. So I wouldn't be surprised if it takes more than an email to get through to them."

"Still, it's a start," Dag said optimistically.

They'd made it safely into town by then, and as he pulled into a parking spot near the ice skating rink, there didn't seem to be more to say on the situation. Plus there was so much going on in the town square that that was where their attention naturally turned.

"After that blizzard yesterday, I can't believe this is all still going on and so many people showed up," Shannon observed.

"One of the advantages of a small town—there aren't a lot of streets to clean so the plow can take care of most of them in a day, and no one has to go too far to get around."

Before they left the heat of the truck's interior, Shannon buttoned the top of her wool coat, tied her knitted scarf around her neck and put on her earmuffs and then her gloves.

Dag fastened a few of his suede coat's buttons and added fleece-lined gloves, but that was as far as he went in bundling up.

Then they got out of the truck.

"According to the schedule in the newspaper this morning," Dag said, "we have a little while before the ice-sculpting competition—I understand there will be chain saws for that so we don't want to miss it—"

Shannon laughed at his enthusiasm for the chain saws. "No, we definitely wouldn't want to miss that!" she agreed, as if it were of the utmost importance.

Dag took the teasing in stride and merely grinned at her. "So we can either wander through the booths before that and then take the sleigh ride, or we can take the sleigh ride before the contest and walk through the booths after—your choice."

"Well, since I'm still warm from the truck, let's do the sleigh ride first. Then we can get under some of the heat lights to watch the chain saw ice massacre and walk through the booths."

"Good choice," Dag decreed.

Shannon had put both of her hands into her coat pockets and without warning, Dag hooked his arm through one of her elbows as if he'd done it a million times before.

And that was all it took for her to feel an instant sense that all was right with the world. Especially when he used their entwined arms to tug her close to his side as they headed for the line of sleighs waiting for passengers.

Confused and somewhat in awe of the phenomena, she glanced up at him, wondering exactly what was going on with her when it came to this man.

But there were no answers in the profile of his handsome face above the turned-up collar of his coat. She just felt another wave of gladness to be there with him.

Maybe it's only the spirit of the holiday, she told herself.

But despite making a valiant attempt to believe that, she still had the sneaking suspicion that it was the man himself.

"We want that one," Dag announced to the teenagers waiting to drive the sleighs that were different in size, shape and ornateness, but all painted white and decorated festively with red ribbons and wreaths on the backsides.

Dag's pick was a simple, plain-sided, old-fashioned country sleigh with a thick plaid wool blanket waiting in its plush red velvet interior.

Once they were situated side by side behind the driver, Dag tucked the blanket around their laps and the driver gently tapped the reins to put the big roan into motion, setting off the jangle of small golden bells on the harness's girth.

The sleigh ride took them in a big circle around the town square and the connecting grounds of the small private college that was closed for winter break.

Dag explained that two other contests had been held—one for the best decorated evergreen tree in the square or on the campus, and another for the best snow sculpture.

"It's no wonder they're offering sleigh rides to see it all," Shannon said in astonishment at what the small town had produced.

Businesses, clubs and organizations had sponsored the decoration of the trees and each one was more elaborate than the other. The tree done by the local beauty salon had won first prize with bedazzled ribbons tied around almost every branch, bright lights and hair accessories all turned into sparkling tree ornaments.

Between the trees done up in festive finery there were snow forts, a snow village, snow families, snow space-ships, snow cathedrals and so many other snow-erected marvels that Shannon lost track of them all.

"This town is just its own little oasis, isn't it?" she said when their sleigh ride tour came to an end.

"Ya gotta love Northbridge," Dag agreed, heading them for the ice-sculpting contest that was getting under way.

Huge blocks of ice had been set up near the gazebo. The contestants went three at a time with a goal of producing the best sculpture in the shortest amount of time.

The expertise in the wielding of the chain saws was something to see all on its own but the little wonder-land of ice sculptures that resulted from it was an added bonus. The sculptures went from simple—a Christmas tree and a snowman—all the way to a complicated castle and even a five-foot-high lumberjack, complete with his dog at his feet.

It was the lumberjack that won and, along with the applause and cheers of the onlookers, the other sculptors did a good-natured chain saw salute to the winner before Shannon and Dag moved on to the booths.

Food, drinks, gifts, ornaments—the bazaar had a different tone than what they'd seen on Main Street on Sunday. Of course there was the hot chocolate and hot cider booth, but there was also a booth that offered Christmas Treats from Around The World—different cookies, desserts and sweets that were traditional to assorted countries and cultures.

There was a booth selling beautiful gingerbread houses for those without the time or inclination to make their own, there was a booth selling hand-carved and painted nativities and another offering all sizes of Moravian stars. There were two stands selling handmade candles, one offering adult-size rocking horses, and several others where hand-knit sweaters and scarves could be had.

All in all, Shannon continued to admire the talents and what seemed like the unlimited energy of the people who lived in Northbridge. But after a few hours, not even the heat lamps were enough to keep away the cold and she was ready to go home.

The problem with that was the thought of saying good-night to Dag—which she wasn't ready to do yet despite all the reasoning she did with herself about why she should be.

So, hoping she wasn't being too transparent, she developed a sudden enthusiasm for the mulled wine being

sold at one stand, bought a bottle and used it as the ex-
cuse to invite Dag back to the apartment—for the third
night in a row—in order not to have this evening end
yet.

And if Dag saw through it?

Shannon couldn't have cared less because he jumped
at the idea, looping his arm through hers as he took her
back to his truck to drive them home.

"Sooo, I'm not engaged and you said last night that
that makes me a free agent," Shannon said forty-five
minutes later when she and Dag were sitting on the
apartment's sofa, in front of a blazing fire in the fireplace, sipping mulled wine.

"Uh-huh," Dag said, an amused but confused frown
pulling his brows together since she had said that out of
the blue.

Shannon was sitting in the middle of the couch, her
feet tucked to one side and underneath her so she could
look at him. Dag was sitting next to her, angled in her
direction, one long arm stretched across the top of the
sofa back.

"And you also said last night that you're a free agent,
too…" she added.

"Did I?"

She might have been more concerned about that question except that the look of mischief in his expression let
her know he was just giving her a hard time.

"You did," she confirmed. "With some conviction
behind it—I believe you said, *Oh, I am! Believe me, I
am!*" Although Shannon put even more oomph into his
words than he had and made him laugh.

"Like that? Did I really say it like that?"

"You did," she claimed. "Which is why it has me

wondering—was that *too* much of a protest? Is it not true?"

He laughed. "Oh, it's true. When it comes to women, I am definitely a free agent. And I have been for about two years."

"Two years? Wow, the last one must have really made you gun-shy."

"Actually, it made me crowbar-shy," he said wryly but with an ominous undertone.

Shannon was curious about why a man who looked like Dag did, who was as charming and funny and nice and fun to be with, was without a girlfriend or fiancée or wife. It hadn't occurred to her that by prying a little into the subject she might be opening a can of worms. But she was too curious not to lift the lid anyway.

"I told you about my fiasco with Wes—even though I wasn't supposed to," she said. "You can trust me with yours…"

"Mine was a fiasco but it was no secret—it made a splash, remember?"

"I remember you saying that the end of your hockey career made a splash. What does that have to do with your last relationship?"

"Everything. And it all made the news. But there *was* a sports element to it, so if you came across anything about it you probably didn't pay any attention to it."

"Sorry," she said unapologetically. "But your love life made the sports page? You must have *really* gotten around!"

Dag's laugh this time was wry as he shook his head in denial. "My *love life* was not a sporting event. It made the sports page because I was a name in hockey at the time and so was the jerk who blindsided me."

"That doesn't sound good," Shannon said more seriously.

"Yeah, you could say it wasn't good," he said with enough of an edge to let her know this subject was even more sobering than she'd imagined.

"If you don't want to talk about it, you don't have to," she said, feeling obligated to offer him the option even though her curiosity was growing by the minute.

"Nah, I can talk about it," he said. "I told you, mine *isn't* a secret, it's just not for the faint of heart."

"I'm not faint of heart," she assured.

"Okay, but don't say you weren't warned...." Dag took a drink of his wine. Then he said, "A little short of three years ago I got involved with a woman named Sandra Pierce."

"A hockey groupie?"

"A hockey wife."

Shannon was midsip of her own wine when he said that and her eyes widened over the rim of her glass. She stared at him in shock. "You were involved with someone else's wife?" she said when she'd swallowed her wine.

"No," he answered instantly and firmly. "I would never get involved with anyone else's wife. I'm not even completely comfortable being here drinking wine with you knowing that you're as fresh out of a relationship as you are."

Shannon opted not to address that in favor of hearing his story. "So how was this Sandra person a hockey wife?"

"She was a former hockey wife. I actually met her the night she was out with friends celebrating that her divorce had become final that day."

"Her divorce from another hockey player," Shannon guessed.

"Exactly. She hadn't been married to anyone on my team, she'd divorced a defenseman on the team we had come into town to play the night before. We'd won our game and were out clubbing to celebrate, too."

"And one celebration overlapped the other?"

"A bunch of rowdy hockey players out on the town, a bunch of already-tipsy women cutting loose—paths crossed, we were buying drinks, you know how it goes."

Shannon's social life had always leaned toward moderation, but there had been a few evenings out with friends when she'd witnessed what he was talking about even if she'd shied away from it herself. So she said, "Sure."

"As the night wore on, I sort of paired up with Sandra. I liked her—she was kind of wild and brash, but she was beautiful and smart, too, and we hit it off. The game we'd played and won the night before had been an exhibition game in Canada but Sandra was from Detroit and she was moving back. We arranged to have dinner when she got there."

"Which you did," Shannon said.

"Which we did. And I still liked her even when she was sober, so we started dating."

"Because you were a free agent then, too, and since she was divorced, so was she."

"That's what I thought. Divorce seems pretty final to me. But I didn't factor in that while things might be over on paper, that doesn't necessarily mean they're *over-over*...."

"Oh-oh…"

"She kept *saying* it was over. But he still called her and she still called him. She'd always tell me whenever they talked so I thought that proved she didn't have anything to hide. I figured it was just an amiable divorce. I didn't think they were talking because they weren't really done with each other—"

"But they weren't."

"I learned later that the calls were mostly about how her ex wanted her back. And that she was torn and actually thinking about it. I was six months into things when she let that slip. If I'd had any brains I would have said goodbye on the spot."

"But you didn't?"

"I didn't," he answered with self-disgust. "I had feelings for her by then. And much to my regret, my competitive streak came right to the surface. Instead of bowing out, I did everything I could think of to win. To get her to pick me over the ex."

The low, disgusted tone of his voice, the way his brows almost met in a frown, let Shannon see how much he damned that choice.

"It didn't work? She picked the ex anyway?" she asked gently.

He shook his head again. He let out a mirthless laugh. He took a drink of his wine and stared at the fire for a moment before he looked Shannon in the eye again and said, "Yeah, she picked the ex anyway, but not until after he and four of his teammates jumped me one night."

Shannon hadn't realized until that moment just how literal he'd meant his comment about crowbars and being blindsided. "Were you alone? Against five other hockey players?"

"I was alone. Coming home after a game, figuring to shower and go over to Sandra's place. Then out of the shadows came these guys…" He shook his head again and he looked more angry than anything as he went on. "I can take a beating with the best of them, and I've dished out plenty of my own on the ice—I played hockey, after all. But these guys took me by surprise—"

"And you were *alone* against *five* of them? With *crowbars?*"

"Sandra's ex-husband was the only one with a crowbar. His four friends held me down while he broke my knee and my leg in three places."

Shannon felt her own eyes widen and the color drain from her face, and she wondered if she might be more fainthearted than she'd thought. "Oh, my god…"

"Luckily a neighbor heard the attack and called the cops—they were there before Sandra's ex got started on the other leg. The cops arrested him and got an ambulance there right away—"

"But the damage he'd already done—"

"Ended my career."

"And hurt you!"

"Five surgeries to put pins in bones and rebuild my knee almost from the ground up. In and out of the hospital, then in and out of rehab each time to make sure the leg would go back to working. I got hit on Christmas Eve the Christmas before last, so I was in the hospital for that one, and I was in rehab after a surgery last Christmas—he definitely did damage."

"No wonder you're so happy to be here this year!"

"And walking."

"But that was it for hockey," Shannon said, referring to his end-of-his-career comment.

"I worked like crazy in rehab every time, thinking I could get back to where I was if I did it with the same intensity I used to train for hockey. But all the doctors, the physical therapists, and then the coaches and trainers and the team doc agreed—there was no way the leg or the knee wouldn't crumble with a good hard hit on the ice. So I had to retire."

He seemed determined not to make it sound like a tragedy, but Shannon knew it had to have been devastating. Still, his refusal to feel sorry for himself reminded her of her parents and all the times she'd watched them put a happy face on their failing health, and she couldn't help being impressed by that in Dag, too.

"What about the creep who did it?" she asked.

"He got eighteen months in jail for assault, his cohorts did a few months each. There was also a civil lawsuit that I filed against them. And won."

"And Sandra?"

"She took the whole thing as some kind of grand romantic gesture," Dag said with disbelief. "It was actually the other guy's winning goal—they remarried the week he was released from jail."

"And you thought that woman was smart?" Shannon said, her own outrage sounding.

"Apparently not when it came to relationships," he admitted.

Shannon glanced at his legs—one of them bent at the knee, his foot on the floor, the other stretched out to the coffee table. She'd never seen him so much as limp and had no idea which leg had ever been hurt.

"It's that one," he said as if he knew what she was thinking, pointing to the leg stretched onto the coffee table.

"How about now—are you okay?"

"For everything but hockey, I'm fine. So I've moved on to the next stage of my life—back to Northbridge and new things here."

And he sounded as if he'd genuinely accepted that without bitterness.

"You're kind of something, you know that?" she heard herself say as she gazed at the face that hockey playing hadn't scarred, as she saw more of the depth of the man and admired his inner strength as much as his outer, his spirit and his ability to take something awful that had happened to him and make the best of it.

"*Kind of something* what?" he asked with a dash of devilry to his voice and to the one eyebrow he raised rakishly at her.

It made Shannon smile. "Just kind of something," she hedged, setting her glass on the coffee table.

Dag did the same with his as he persisted, "Kind of something wonderful? Kind of something brave and heroic? Kind of something too hot to resist?"

All of the above, Shannon thought.

But she didn't say it. She just laughed at him because it was obvious he was joking. "I'll give you brave—because even after that you're still here with me when I'm as fresh out of a relationship as I am," she said, reiterating his earlier words.

"Well, yeah, that *is* brave," he deadpanned. "Facing down five hockey thugs is one thing, but a politician? I could end up with my taxes raised or an IRS audit—that's *really* terrifying!"

Shannon laughed again, also appreciating his sense of humor.

Then he said, "You're not going to offer to kiss it and make it better?"

"Your knee? No. Have you had a lot of offers to do that?"

"One or two—nurses can be hockey fans, too, you know."

"Then you don't need me to do it, do you?"

"Need? Maybe not…" he said, bringing his hand up from the sofa back to cup the side of her face. "But want? That's another subject…"

"Even under threat of higher taxes and audits?" she asked, her voice somehow just barely above an inviting whisper as she lost herself a little in black eyes that were delving into hers.

"Even then…" he said, coming forward enough to kiss her—but so lightly it was more like the kiss he'd pressed to her hand than the one they'd shared the night before and she wondered if he was a little leery after all.

If he was, it didn't last, though, because after a moment he deepened the kiss, parting his lips and hers, and slipping his hand to the back of her head, into her hair while his other hand came to the other side of her neck, inside the collar of the blouse she wore under a V-necked sweater.

He had the warmest hands. And a touch that only hinted at the power they contained as his lips parted wider still and his tongue came to meet hers.

Shannon's own hands rose to his solid chest, once again encased in a plaid flannel shirt over a thermal T-shirt. She wished there were fewer layers between them as their kiss rapidly escalated, mouths opening wider and tongues courting and cavorting.

Dag's arms came around her then, pulling her so close she was nearly lying across his lap, held by those massive arms as he took that kiss to yet another level. A level that was so thoroughly intimate it was almost an act of love all on its own.

It most definitely awakened things in Shannon that no mere kiss ever had. She was suddenly aware of every inch of her skin, of a craving to be set free of her shirt, her sweater, her jeans. Her breasts seemed to swell, testing the confines of her bra, begging for the touch of more than lace. Her knees pressed together to contain the desires that sprang to life in places that should have been sleeping. And until they were already there, she didn't even realize that her arms had gone around Dag's broad shoulders or that her fingers were digging into his back.

And that ravaging kiss just fed it all like fuel. She gave as good as she got—plundering his mouth as surely as he plundered hers, with an abandon that would have shocked the politician even after years together. An abandon that the hockey player took in stride.

But it was that abandon that actually gave Shannon pause, that gave her the sense that she was somehow not herself, that warned her to slow down, to think, to stop before things went too far...

She slid her hands from Dag's back to his muscle-wrapped rib cage, then to his chest again. But instead of pushing him away, she continued caressing those perfect pectorals for a while, almost forgetting herself all over again. Until she realized what was about to happen and then she put some effort into taming the kiss, finally managing to begin a retreat.

Dag got the message, although he showed no eagerness to end anything and even after tongues had parted ways, he still kissed her and kissed her again. And kissed her once more on the side of her neck where he flicked the tip of his tongue just a little.

After another moment of nuzzling her neck, he rose up enough to rest his chin atop her head and sigh. "Okay," he said as if she'd spoken. "I s'pose we should call it a night."

"I think it's late..." Shannon said by way of agreement.

Another sigh. "Yeah, probably is…"

Still they stayed the way they were—his arms wrapping her, cradling her, her head against his shoulder.

"I know you hate sports," Dag said then. "But tomorrow night the local men's team plays their Christmas basketball game, and the school choir is singing carols at halftime. From what I hear nearly everyone in town is going. Can I persuade you—even if Logan and Meg and Chase and Hadley decide not to?"

At that moment Shannon thought he could persuade her to go to the moon with him.

"While I'm here I might as well get the full Northbridge experience," she said as if that was the only reason.

"You might as well."

He kissed the top of her head, and Shannon closed her eyes, drinking in the feel of his breath in her hair before she sat up to really let him go.

Then they both got off the couch and Dag shrugged back into his coat as they headed for the door.

There didn't seem to be anything to say but goodnight, and that's what they did. Afterward Dag stood there for a moment looking down at her.

She thought he was considering kissing her again. Or maybe fighting not to. But either way, he didn't. He merely repeated his good-night and left.

Which was for the best, Shannon told herself.

Because the kissing they'd already done had gotten a little out of control and she wasn't sure if even a simple kiss at the door might have started it all over again.

And if a part of her wished it might have? Wished it had started all over again and gone so, so much further?

That was the part of her that she hadn't really known existed until tonight.

A part of her that she found unnerving, unsettling…

And maybe a little more exciting than she knew what to do with.

Chapter Ten

"Three shopping days until Christmas and I haven't even *started* yet!"

"Then what are you doing on the phone with me instead of hitting the mall?" Shannon responded, when she answered her friend Danica Bond's call early Wednesday morning. She followed it with a belated, "Hi, Dani."

"Hi, Shan. I haven't talked to you since you left for Northbridge. I just wanted to check in, see how you're doing—*then* I'm hitting the mall."

"I'm doing really well," Shannon said. "Much better than I expected, actually. It's like something out of a Christmas movie here and it's nice spending time with Chase and Hadley and Cody. Chase and I have even found out what family the twins ended up with...." She went on to explain how her younger brothers were part of the Kincaid family.

"And why haven't I heard a public announcement yet that you and Wes aren't engaged?" Dani asked then.

Dani was the one person on Shannon's side—before Dag—who was aware that there wasn't an engagement. Shannon had told Dani in advance that she was going to break up with Wes so Dani hadn't ever believed that Shannon had accepted the proposal. Plus she and Shannon had talked several times since then and Dani knew exactly what was going on. But she, too, had sworn to keep quiet.

"Wes is dragging his feet," Shannon said.

"But he hasn't worn you down, has he?"

"No, he hasn't worn me down. He's trying, but not nearly hard enough. Every reason he gives me to marry him is still about votes and voters. He can be really clueless sometimes."

But Wes was the last thing that Shannon wanted to talk about so she said, "What about you—have you honestly not even started Christmas shopping yet?"

"I honestly haven't. I've been too swamped with the school—there's even a temporary sign up now that says Coming Soon: The Early Childhood Development Center. I can't wait for you to get here after Christmas and see everything. We're about three-quarters finished with construction so it's easy to envision the way it will look in the end—just like the drawing I sent you from the architect. Only in real life it's much more impressive. You're going to love it! You're going to love California, too, and never want to leave—I just know it! I can't wait for you to *finally* get here!"

Dani's enthusiasm was infectious and it made Shannon smile. She missed her friend. Because of her own job and caring for her parents, she hadn't been able to visit Dani in Beverly Hills, and Dani hadn't come back to Montana nearly often enough since marrying Ronald Bond two years before and leaving. She had come back for all three funerals during the last year but each of those trips had had to be quick and she and Shannon hadn't spent any real time together.

"I have your room ready," Dani went on, "and it would be fine with me if you got here, decided to come on board with the school and just never left."

Shannon laughed. "I would still have to come back to Billings and move my stuff."

"Okay, one trip and that's all," Dani said. "Because nobody can tell me that once I get you here it isn't going to hit you that *this* is how you can break out and move on to bigger and better things—the way we talked about when we were kids, the way we dreamed about, the way I have."

It never failed that when she talked to Dani about moving to Beverly Hills, about going in on the school with her old friend, Shannon was always tempted to just say *Sign me up!*

But even without the possibility of a future with Wes holding her back, she still didn't do that. Her parents had lived a cautious life—financially and otherwise—and she supposed they'd passed on the need for caution to her. As a result, despite the lure of what Dani was offering, Shannon knew she had to see things for herself, get a feel for the school, for California and Beverly Hills, and seriously consider everything before she committed to anything. Even if Dani was involved.

So she merely said, "I can't wait to see you."

"But you're really doing okay? I mean…the first Christmas without everybody…"

"I'm a little blue here and there." She admitted to her friend what she hadn't said to anyone else. "But everyone is so nice and the whole town is—"

"Don't let it suck you in!" Dani ordered.

"Did I say it was sucking me in?"

"I can hear something in your voice—you like it there. Or have you met someone…"

Dani knew her much, much too well. "My brother's partner's brother—Dag—is helping to show me around, but it isn't as if I've *met someone*, no," Shannon insisted.

Although that somehow felt like a lie. Especially when the image of Dag came so vividly to mind suddenly and sent a wave of warmth all through her. Warmth and the same eagerness to be with him again that she felt every minute they were apart…

"Well, don't let him suck you in, either," Dani said. "This is your time and don't let anyone keep you from having it."

Ah, but Dani hadn't met Dag.

And she certainly hadn't been kissed by him the way he'd kissed Shannon the night before.…

"You know my coming out there after Christmas doesn't make this a done deal," Shannon felt obligated to remind her friend then. "As much as I hate that you moved away and as much as I'd like us to be near each other again—"

"I know," Dani interrupted her. "I won't blame you if investing in the school seems too scary—without Ron I wouldn't be brave enough… Well, without Ron I wouldn't be able to do it at all since most of the capital is his. But I've been thinking and even if you don't want to jump in right away, you can still think about just giving me a year—"

"A year?"

"You could set up the pre-K and kindergarten section, and when school starts in the fall, you could teach here instead of in Montana. It would give you a chance to try it all out. You wouldn't even have to get a place, you could stay with Ron and me and just settle in temporarily to make up your mind. You can even invest after that, if you want to. Once you see that we can make a go of it, it will ease your mind."

It was an offer too good to refuse.

Yet Shannon still said, "We'll talk about it when I get there."

"Oh, believe me, I'm talking about it until I get you to say yes!"

Shannon laughed at her friend. "Now *that's* the kind of determination Wes should have had."

"Isn't that the truth!" Dani agreed.

"Anyway," Shannon said then, "for now I'm due to bake and decorate Christmas cookies with Hadley, Meg and Tia. And you'd better go shopping."

"That's where I'm headed. I probably won't bother you again until Christmas day. But if you get too blue—day or night—you call me, okay?"

Shannon knew Dani meant that. The same way she would always be available to Dani day or night. "Okay," Shannon agreed. "But go on—shop. And happy hunting."

"At this point there's no time for hunting—I'm rushing in, buying and rushing on to the next store!"

While Chase and Logan helped Dag with some woodwork at Dag's place that afternoon, Shannon went to the main house to pitch in with the Christmas cookie making, and to lend Meg and Hadley a hand with Tia and Cody.

There was discussion between Meg and Hadley about whether or not to attend the evening's basketball game that Dag had asked Shannon to, but in the end the other two women decided on another quiet evening in.

Obviously since Chase and Hadley were newlyweds, and Meg and Logan had only been married a few months, at that point nothing was quite as compelling for either of the two couples as time alone.

Meg and Hadley did encourage Shannon to go, however, and Shannon told herself she should do it for the sake of her brother and his bride, to give them that time alone.

Which seemed like a much better reason than that she might just want to be with Dag the same way Hadley and Meg wanted to be with Chase and Logan.

So after a quick dinner with Chase, Hadley and Cody at the loft, Shannon rushed back to the apartment to change into her best butt-hugging tan slacks. Gambling that it might not be warm enough, she nonetheless put on a U-necked T-shirt over a tight camisole top that gave her enough lift to form the hint of cleavage. Then she freshened her blush and mascara before she took her hair out of the ponytail it had been in all day and brushed it to fall free around her shoulders.

But again she swore to herself that sprucing up wasn't for Dag, that it was only because she was going out for the evening.

As planned, at six forty-five, she heard Dag drive his truck around to the garage to get her. She was just putting on her coat and tying a matching scarf around her neck when he knocked on the door.

Opening it to him, she could tell that he'd put a little extra thought into his own attire tonight, too. He had on a very dashing-looking calf-length black wool coat over a pair of charcoal-colored slacks that fit him so well they had to have been specially made to accommodate his hockey player thighs. He also had on a cashmere polo-style sweater that caressed his upper body in a way that made Shannon's hands want to do the same thing.

He was freshly shaven, his almost-black hair was shiny-clean and artfully disarrayed, and all in all, he had more of an air of a take-charge corporate raider than a jock or a cowboy. And were Shannon to hazard a guess, she would have said that that was how he had dressed to go out clubbing after hockey games when groupies had gathered and—no doubt—swooned at the transformation he was capable of making. She, herself, certainly had to put a whole lot of effort into not swooning....

"This is a good look for you," she mentioned casually when she realized she was staring and mentally kicked herself.

Dag merely smiled, gave her an up-and-down glance and said, "I haven't seen a look that isn't good on you yet."

Then he swiveled away from blocking the door and with a sweep of his arm, he invited her to go ahead of him out of the apartment.

The basketball game was being played in the school gymnasium by the local men's team that played baseball, basketball and football against each other year-round. But despite the loud and jocular participation of the crowd, despite the humor and festiveness exhibited by the players in the holly crowns, the bell-adorned wrist-bands, and the red-and-white or green-and-white striped knee socks they wore to designate teams, Shannon was no more enthralled with this sport than with any other.

She liked the choir concert of Christmas carols sung by the school children at halftime, but she was glad when Dag suggested they leave after that.

"I'm sorry if I was a drag," she apologized as they

left the school. "I just can't begin to tell you how sports-stupid I am and it's hard to get into something when I honestly don't have any idea what I'm watching."

Dag leaned sideways and said, "To tell you the truth, I didn't make it back to Logan's for dinner tonight and I'm starving. I thought I might be able to persuade you to grab some takeout with me and go back to your place for a bite to eat. That's what I was fantasizing about through "Silent Night"—you, me, another fire and a burger."

Shannon had to laugh at the rapture with which he'd said *burger*. "Even though I came first on that list, why do I still get the feeling that the hamburger is the biggest draw?" she teased him.

He grinned. "Low self-esteem?"

"That must be it," Shannon said facetiously before she agreed to his suggestion.

A quick stop at the Tastee Dog's new drive-through window and within fifteen minutes they were back at Shannon's place with Shannon taking a turn at building a fire while Dag ate.

Then they were once again where Shannon secretly most wanted to be—sitting on the center of the sofa in front of that fire. Alone, together...

"So what did you think of our school, Ms. Kindergarten Teacher?" Dag asked as they began to share the brownie-mint ice cream sundae that was the dessert Shannon had agreed to partake in.

"I didn't see much of it," Shannon said.

There were three buildings that housed it—one each for the elementary, middle and high school grade levels—and Shannon had only seen the gym. Since that was also the site for the elementary grades, she *had* seen the kindergarten classroom.

"It looks like a nice school, though," she said. "For such a small area I'm kind of surprised by how nice it is."

"It probably doesn't compare to whatever is going on in Beverly Hills with your friend's school, but still—"

"It gets the job done," Shannon finished for him. Then she said, "I actually talked to my friend Dani this morning. She says her school is shaping up."

"And that it could all be yours?"

"Not all of it, no. But a small piece of the pie."

"So I'm curious," Dag said as they finished the sundae, set the container on the coffee table and moved on to the spicy tea Shannon had brewed for them. "This Dani is your best friend, right? You're not marrying the Rumson. You've sold your parents' business and the building that was home to you all. You've sold your grandmother's house here. It seems like you've cut all the ties in Montana in order to move on and that you kind of like the idea of going out to California with your friend. But you haven't actually made that decision?"

"I didn't sell anything to *cut ties,*" Shannon amended his assumption. "I had to sell the business and the building it was in to pay off the last of my parents' medical bills. I wasn't going to move to Northbridge to live, so there wasn't a reason to keep Gramma's house—especially since I couldn't afford any kind of upkeep or the taxes or insurance on it. And between what little was left of my parents' assets after the bills and the sale of Gramma's place, that still only gave me a small nest egg."

"But now you have that nest egg and it gives you the money to invest," Dag said, putting his mug of tea on the coffee table after a few sips.

Shannon went on warming her hands around her cup. "Yes. But if I invest the nest egg, then no nest egg," she said reasonably. "And if the investment doesn't pay off, I won't have anything. Nothing. No job to go back to—because right now I'm on sabbatical and slated to return to work next fall, but if I don't do that, I'm giving up my job. Also if I move to California and The Early Childhood Development Center doesn't succeed, it isn't as if I have parents to help out or come back to."

"But it isn't as if you're alone in the world—you have Chase, he's your brother," Dag reminded.

And Shannon didn't doubt that if she needed Chase's help, he would give it. But still their relationship was in the infant stages and asking him for help—especially financial—wasn't something she actually felt she could do. It was certainly something she wouldn't want to do.

"And I'd still have Dani," she pointed out, thinking aloud, sorting through the pros and cons with Dag and wondering at the fact that she *did* feel comfortable doing that with him.

"Unless owning a business together and working together put a strain on the friendship," he said. "Or doesn't that worry you?"

"It does…" she said, but she hadn't had anyone to talk to about it and now that Dag had brought it up, she appreciated the chance to air her feelings.

"Dani and I have been friends since we were kids," Shannon said. "We're as close as I imagine sisters are. I'd do anything for her and I know she would do anything for me—"

"Why do I hear a *but* coming?"

"But we're different, Dani and I. We have different ways of doing things, different temperaments, different opinions. It's never mattered before because we always went our own directions—even though Dani's a teacher, too, she's taught fourth, fifth or sixth grade because she says the ages below that are too immature for her. We've always shared what we had in common and supported each other when either of us did something the other one didn't, but—"

"If you invest in the school—"

"And/or go to work there, that's something we've never done before."

"It might be fine—"

"Or it might mess up our friendship. And I don't know if anything is worth that," Shannon confided.

Dag nodded his understanding. Before he'd said anything, however, she went on with her list of pros and cons.

"Plus there's Dani's husband…" she whispered as if someone else might hear as she finished her tea and set the mug on the coffee table beside Dag's.

"You don't like him?"

"He's…" She shrugged while she chose her words, not wanting to say too much against her best friend's spouse. "He's kind of full of himself and maybe just a little…slick. He needs to be the center of attention—the smartest, most successful person in the room. And he's the major investor in the school—which still makes it Dani's school since she's his wife, but I know that everything has to have his okay on it. I don't know if that's just for now—in terms of construction—or if it's going to influence the way things are done with the kids, with the educational programs. I just don't know how far his input and influence are going to go."

"That seems like something to find out before you get in," Dag counseled.

"There's also the fact that it will be a private school in *Beverly Hills,*" Shannon went on because now that she'd started this, she thought she might as well get it all out. "I've only worked in public school. I don't know if

I'll fit in, if I'll feel uncomfortable or out of my element there. I don't know if a schoolteacher—even in a private school—is a respected part of a community like that or not. I just don't know if I'll like it. And if I don't and all my money is tied up in it, then what? Then I'm back to the financial issues and having no one...."

"Or then maybe you just cash in on your investment and make another change," he suggested. "You could even come back here. I could keep a room for you, if you want. I'll put a plaque on the door that says The Just-In-Case Room of Shannon Duffy. Would that help?"

Shannon laughed. "You're kidding, but I might take you up on it."

"Who says I'm kidding?" he asked with a kind smile. "I can keep the cubbyhole room for you."

"Why do I think you actually might do that if I asked you to?"

"Because I would?"

Maybe he wasn't joking.

"I'm sure the future Mrs. Dag McKendrick would love that!" Shannon said.

"*Future* is the key word—if there *is* a future Mrs. Dag McKendrick, then we can make adjustments. But until then? I'll be your safety net if you'd feel better knowing you literally have a place to come back to if Beverly Hills doesn't work out."

"You're serious..." Shannon said when she began to believe he was.

"I am," he answered as if he'd made the decision on the spot but was willing to run with it. "Let me sign on to be your safety net."

Oddly enough, that had an appeal because she somehow did feel safe with this man. Among so many other things she felt about him and with him...

But she tried not to think too much about those feelings and to stick to reality.

"It would be weird to go to Chase for help," she said then, "but you think it would be less weird to go to the brother of my brother's partner for it?"

"Why is it weird if I'm volunteering? It can be like a pact we make, one free agent to another free agent—if I get sick of Northbridge and long for the Hills of Beverly, I'll come to you—"

"We both know that isn't going to happen, you *love* it here."

He shrugged that off and went on with the terms of his pact. "And if things don't work out for you there, you'll come to me. I sort of like the idea of being someone you'd turn to if you needed to."

She sort of liked that idea, too. But she wasn't sure why. "Thanks, but—"

Dag took her hand, holding it, rubbing the back of it with his thumb in a way that was an enticement all its own. "Just factor it into your thinking," he said then. "Maybe it'll help you make your decision—if Beverly Hills still seems too risky even when you have a backup plan, then you may realize that isn't the way to go. If you feel more free to jump in *because* you have a backup plan, then maybe you should give it a try. I've heard that sometimes just having the safety net in place makes the high-wire walker less likely to fall."

"You dated a circus performer?" she joked to hide how touched she was by his willingness to make things easier for her.

His smile was simple and sweet and endearing. "Only for a little while," he said, his voice deeper, more quiet suddenly as he went on rubbing her hand with his thumb, watching himself do it, unaware of the tiny electrical charges it was sending up her arm.

Then he raised her hand to kiss it much the way he had those other nights. Except unlike those other nights, once he'd kissed it, he let go of it and raised his palm to the side of her neck, and met her gaze with his dark, smoldering eyes.

"Not that I'm advocating for you to leave," he said just before he closed the distance between them and took her mouth with his.

Why that kiss was like coming home, Shannon had no idea. But there was such warm familiarity in lips parted instantly to perfection, in mouths that seemed to fit together as if one had been carved from the other, and she just melted into that kiss.

Her palms rose to his cashmere-covered chest the way they'd been aching to do since the minute she'd laid eyes on him tonight. His other arm came around her, pulling her closer, repositioning them both so they were facing each other on the sofa.

The kiss deepened, reawakening that part of her that she'd discovered the night before, inviting it to come out to play again.

She could feel that slightly wilder streak rising, gaining ground, with each circle and thrust of Dag's talented tongue, with each time her own met and matched it. And when his hand went to the back of her head to brace it for the deepening of that kiss, when he held her tighter, she didn't think she could have contained herself even if she'd wanted to.

The man just brought things to life in her! As if every sense was on high alert—but only in the best way. With Dag, kissing wasn't merely kissing, it was an indulgence in something decadent, and every movement, every placement of his hands in her hair, on her back, between her shoulder blades, only made her want to feel them everywhere else, too.

Her nipples grew taut behind the binding knit of the camisole that held them confined and thoughts of those big hands on her breasts suddenly became inescapable. Those big, strong hands...

She massaged the muscles of his broad back, which barely gave way beneath her fingers digging ardently through his sweater. The sweater that—regardless of how soft and fine it felt—stood between her and his bare flesh.

The new, more daring Shannon found the bottom of his sweater and slipped her hands underneath it, sliding them up sleek skin over honed muscle as Dag came slightly more atop her, his mouth pillaging hers as his hand found her breast, surprising and delighting her at once.

But both the surprise and the delight were short-lived because Shannon wanted so much to feel his hand on her bare flesh that she could have ripped her shirts off herself.

Dag always seemed somehow in tune with her and no sooner had that thought flitted through her mind than he snaked his hand under both shirts and found her naked breasts.

First one, then the other, giving them both equal time, equal opportunity to know the magic of a touch that was, by turns, light and firm, playful and serious, teasing and tormenting.

It felt so wonderful that Shannon's breath caught in a tiny gasp and all new desires made themselves known, causing her to slip one of her legs over his.

Desires that only mounted when his mouth left hers,

kissing, nibbling a trail down her neck, to her side, to her belly and then up to take her breast into that sweet haven.

The wild streak in her took full hold then and thrust her forward without inhibition, begging for more of that hot, wet wonder of mouth and tongue and teeth that stole her breath and left her weak with all the more wanting.

Because yes, she did want this man more than she'd ever wanted any man!

So much more that again it was a little alarming...

What if this was just some kind of rebound thing? What if it was some kind of insanity that had come from so much loss? What if it was some kind of seizing-of-life after so many encounters with death?

But it might just be Dag, she thought as he drew her breast more deeply into his mouth, as his tongue did a twirl around her nipple and it seemed as if it was Dag and Dag alone that she wanted.

It might just be Dag...

And how special, how cared for, he made her feel. How free...

But freedom was one of the things she'd always thought came with a bigger life. That brought Beverly Hills to mind to add to her qualms.

Beverly Hills and a bigger life and the fact that living in Northbridge—the way Dag did and was determined to do from here on—was not a life she had ever dreamed of.

Which screamed for her to keep things cool with him.

Too late for that, she thought because she was already on fire for him.

But still once the reasonable, rational side of her

recognized that she should cool this off, it wouldn't leave her alone. And as amazing as kissing him was, as amazing as it was to have his hands on her, to have his mouth on her breast, she didn't think she could let it go on…

No matter how much she wanted it to.

And oh, did she want it to!

But other than what was happening at that moment, they wanted different, different things. So wanting him, wanting what he was doing to her, had to be sacrificed.

Yes, the small groan that echoed from her throat then was in response to a tiny flick of his tongue to the very tip of her nipple and how good it felt. But it was also to her own decision that she couldn't have more of that. Of Dag. And it was that decision that made her draw back just enough to let him know not to go on. That decision that dropped her head to the top of the couch cushion as Dag got the hint and stopped.

His audible exhalation was disappointed but resolved. He pulled her shirts down and then her head to rest on his chest so that he could lower his cheek to it.

And this time it seemed as if she had an inkling of what he was thinking even before he whispered in a gravely voice, "Yeah, you're right, we shouldn't."

Shannon had no explanation whatsoever for why Dag thinking that, too, should disappoint her. But she wrote it off to the confusion of emotions that were all running rampant through her at that moment, and agreed. "No, we shouldn't."

Yet they stayed the way they were for a while longer, holding each other, in no hurry to part.

But it had to be done and eventually it was Dag

who did it—sending another wave of regret through Shannon.

Dag raised his head from hers, loosening his arms from around her, sitting up straighter. She sat up, too.

He kissed her again. Briefly. As if he just couldn't stop himself. Then he stood, swiped his coat from the arm of the nearby chair and put it on while Shannon got to her feet to walk him to the door.

He kissed her yet again there—his hands were shoved into his coat pockets so he didn't touch her, but the kiss was still long and lingering and open mouthed, a sexy farewell that made Shannon hate that there was any farewell being said at all.

But just when she was fighting the inclination to ask him to stay, he ended that kiss, too, straightened up again and glanced over her head at the apartment.

"I think tomorrow we need to get a little Christmas cheer into this place," he decreed. "What do you say we cut you a tree and decorate it?"

The man just always made her smile....

"Isn't that a lot of work for just a couple of days until it's all over?"

"A couple of days is still a couple of days that you'll get to have it," he said, looking at her again and making her think that it wasn't only a Christmas tree on his mind when he said that.

But one way or another, what he was suggesting would give her more time with him and even though she told herself she shouldn't do it, that he was just too hard for her to resist and that she was tempting fate, she heard herself say, "I've never cut my own Christmas tree...."

"So tomorrow it is?"

"If you don't have anything else to do..."

"I don't have anything else I'd rather do."

He held her eyes with his for another moment. He kissed her again—this time a quick buss. And then he said, "Tomorrow it is," in a husky voice, before he opened the door and went out into the cold.

And not even the blast of winter air that shocked Shannon as she watched him go could cool her off.

Instead, hours and hours after she'd closed the door, changed into her pajamas and gone to bed, she was still feeling the heat of Dag.

And still wanting him every bit as badly as she had when she'd been in his arms.

Chapter Eleven

Cutting down a Christmas tree for the apartment was delayed on Thursday when Chase received an answer to the email he and Shannon had sent to Ian Kincaid.

Shannon ended up spending the morning with Chase, using the phone number in the return email to try to reach Ian.

That eventually happened, leading to a lengthy conference call during which Ian let them know that he and Hutch also had no idea there were other siblings, that he had thought Chase and Shannon's email was some sort of scam until he'd spoken to his mother. Reluctantly, his mother had admitted that there had been another brother and two sisters.

Ian—like Shannon and Chase before him—was thunderstruck. But he had agreed to arrange a time to meet Chase and Shannon after the first of the year.

The second twin—Hutch—was another matter.

Hutch was apparently not on good terms with the Kincaid family. They had not been in touch in several years.

"This is the last email address I have for him, but I haven't used it in so long, I can't tell you that it will get you through to him," Ian said, giving them the address but not offering to relay the news of newfound family himself. And also, Shannon noted, not explaining why a rift existed.

When the phone call ended, Shannon went from Chase's loft to the main house in search of Dag. But Dag had gone into town and left word for her that he would be back soon.

Soon was just after lunch and that was when Shannon bundled up in borrowed heavy-weather gear to go out into the countryside to finally cut her Christmas tree.

The sun was shining, the sky was blue, but it was only three degrees. Shannon wouldn't have blamed Dag if he had backed out of the tree-cutting with the temperature that low, but he was good-natured, full of energy and enthusiasm, and—as usual—game for anything. The only thing he would concede to was not going too far to find a tree.

Luckily there was a stand of evergreens a mere two miles from the barn on Chase and Logan's land, so that was where Dag and Shannon went. Dag parked as near as he could to the small forest but they still had to hike through knee-high snow to reach the trees.

Shannon was grateful when they located one that was a mere four feet high not far into the cluster.

"This one! This is the one," she decreed, breathing warm air into her gloved hands. "Cut it down and let's get out of this cold!"

Dag grinned at her, seeming amused by her chattering

teeth. But he didn't hesitate to use a chain saw at the base of the low-lying fir while Shannon stood back and watched.

And that actually helped with the cold.

The mere sight of the big man, dressed like a burly lumberjack, wielding the saw with expertise, was enough to chase away some of Shannon's chill. Or maybe it was just the fact that she was so enthralled with him that she forgot about the frigid temperature. Instead—as she had so many times since she'd put a stop to it—she relived in vivid detail all that had happened between them the night before. And that was like a little ray of private sunshine heating her from the inside out...

When the tree toppled, Dag bent over, picked it up with one hand and held it in the air as if it were a trophy. "Another brother and a Christmas tree for Shannon Duffy all in one day!" he shouted in victory.

"Let's just get the tree home where there's heat!" Shannon said in response, pretending that Dag didn't generate that for her all on his own.

The remainder of the afternoon went into building a stand for the tree, after which Shannon and Dag joined everyone else at the loft where Hadley had made a dinner of beef stew.

And as much as Shannon enjoyed having so many people around her and being included in the large extended family, tonight she was eager to get away from them all, to get back to the apartment.

Only to put up her Christmas tree, she told herself. It wasn't merely another evening alone with Dag that had her antsy.

Except that visions of Christmas decorations weren't dancing through her head.

Regardless of how much she denied it, it was still Dag who was firmly on her mind....

* * *

"That's what you were doing in town—buying lights and tinsel and ornaments for my tree? I thought I was just using whatever Logan and Chase had left over," Shannon said when she and Dag finally got to the apartment Thursday evening and Dag brought in two sacks full of Christmas decorations that he'd purchased that morning.

"It isn't much. But while you and Chase were talking to Ian Kincaid, I got the bug to go pick up a few things. This stuff will all get used somewhere again next year, so what's the harm?"

There wasn't any harm. In fact it was another nice thing he'd done for her. Another nice, thoughtful thing.

"Let me at least pay for them," she offered.

"Nah. This close to the big day everything was on closeout. Consider it part of your Christmas gift."

"*Part* of my Christmas gift? You got me a Christmas gift?" Shannon couldn't resist saying.

Dag grinned. "Santa brings everybody a Christmas gift," he answered with a wink as he hunkered down to make a fire before they got started.

Try to keep a lid on it, Shannon warned herself when her eyes followed him to the hearth, devouring the sight of him much the way she had that afternoon.

But she wasn't sure she could.

After cutting down the tree and making the stand for it, they'd gone their separate ways to get ready for the evening. For Shannon that had meant a shower and shampoo to get the sawdust off her.

It had also meant some special attention to curling her hair into loose waves around her face, into applying fresh makeup and into opting for her tightest jeans and a teal-green turtleneck that also conformed to her curves. A turtleneck sweater that she'd buttoned up all the way to her chin but that stopped at the exact spot the jean's waistband began so that if she raised her arms the slightest bit, she flashed a hint of skin—unless she wore a tank top underneath it, which she usually did. Except tonight…

Dag had showered, as well. He'd also changed into clean jeans that were low on his hips. And tonight, rather than wearing one of the thermal T-shirts underneath a second shirt, Dag had on the thermal T-shirt alone—a white crewnecked thermal knit that fit like a second skin and left no question that his V-shaped torso was all lean muscle and sinew.

And the fact that he had the long sleeves pushed to his elbows and she could see his forearms? Who would ever believe that one look at those forearms could send a tiny tingle along the surface of her own skin? But it did.

He'd also shaved again before dinner, and combed his hair, and he smelled of that cologne that she attributed to him and him alone. And altogether Shannon knew it was not going to be easy to keep a lid on anything when it came to Dag.

Once the fire was made they went to work on the tree, using an end table to elevate it. All the while they did the job, Dag sang in a surprisingly good voice, making Shannon laugh because his own made-up versions of the old favorite Christmas carols were sometimes a little raunchy and always irreverent.

And when the tree was finished he brought out a bottle of wine he'd also gotten in town that morning, opened it and poured them each a glass.

Then he turned off all the lights so the apartment was

illuminated only by the fire's glow and the tiny twinkling white lights on the tree.

They'd taken off their wet shoes when they'd come in and they sat together in the center of the sofa again, only tonight they were slumped down, both pairs of stockinged feet on the coffee table, heads resting on the back of the couch—to sip wine and look at their handiwork.

"Sooo…I've been wondering about something," Dag said then.

"What?"

"Well, you've mentioned wanting a bigger life a couple of times, but it occurred to me that I'm not quite sure what exactly makes up your idea of that. Is it traveling around the world in a hot air balloon? Climbing Mount Everest? Wiping out illiteracy for all time?"

Shannon laughed. "Traveling, yes—but not necessarily around the *whole* world, just the parts I'd like to see with my own eyes. And definitely not in a hot air balloon, a plane would be just fine. And forget Mount Everest, Montana is cold enough for me. Sure, I'd like to wipe out illiteracy for all time, but I'm happy sending one kindergarten class a year on to first grade with the basics. It isn't as if I have grandiose visions."

"What, then?"

"I guess I mean *bigger* as in broader—not isolated, with more options, more choices for everything. I don't want to always be the person looking at other people's pictures and hearing other people's stories, I want pictures of my own to show, stories of my own to tell. I don't dream of being the first woman to walk on Mars, but I want to be *having* experiences, not just watching them on TV."

"You want more freedom than your parents had, more

than you had, since you had to take care of them. Up
until very recently, your life was bound to theirs."

Shannon hadn't thought of herself as *bound* to her
parents' life, but now that Dag put it into that perspective, she knew she had been.

"You're right," she said. "And in a lot of ways, to me,
I guess having a bigger life means the kind of freedom
most people have and take for granted. It doesn't necessarily have to be full of fanfare, it just has to be…I don't
know, life not lived in a cocoon."

"Like the cocoon of a small town."

"A small town does seem cocoonlike," she agreed.

And she knew that appealed to Dag. But for some
reason, tonight, highlighting where they differed seemed
depressing. Thinking beyond what they had right then,
alone together, talking, enjoying the wine and the fire
and the tree, brought her down. So she changed the
subject.

"Now, what *I've* been wondering about is if you really
did date a circus performer.…"

Dag laughed out loud, heartily, happily, with that
barrel-chested laugh he had. And just the sound of it
made her smile and chased away any doldrums that had
threatened.

"You're wondering if I really dated a circus performer
because of my safety-net-tightrope-walker crack last
night?" he clarified. "As a matter of fact, I *did* date a
circus performer, and she *was* a tightrope walker. And
a contortionist."

"Oh, dear…" Shannon said, thinking that that was
a lot to compete with. If she were competing… "Isn't
that every man's dream?" she asked. "Being with a
contortionist?"

"I don't know about every man's dream, but I know it

got me some high-fives in the locker room. I just didn't admit that I never got her into bed."

"That's not an image I want to think about," Shannon confessed, laughing herself. Then she persisted with what she'd actually been curious about. "But what about serious relationships other than the last one that got you battered—have you had any?"

"Serious? Two, I guess. If serious means thinking and talking about marriage but not actually getting to the engaged phase."

"But close to it?"

"Both times were after a long while of dating—one for a year, the other for almost two—when the women I was involved with decided that was enough of the dating—"

"They proposed to you?"

"Proposed? No, it was more like ultimatums—marry me or we're done."

"So you were done?"

Dag shrugged. "I didn't have marrying kinds of feelings for them. I was sorry about it, sorry to have the relationships end because I liked both Steph and Trish and I enjoyed my time with them. But that's just the way it was—when I tried to picture myself with them forever, I couldn't do it. What about you? Anybody before the Rumson?"

"Two for me, too. But mine were both proposals."

"Really…" he said, raising his eyebrows at her. "And assuming you said no both of those times, too, the Rumson made it *three* guys you turned down? Are you allergic to marriage?"

"No. The first one was my high school sweetheart— he didn't have plans to go to college, he'd already gone through a mechanics training program and was going to work repairing cars as soon as we graduated. He wanted to get married then, too, thought having an apartment over a garage—like our apartment over the shoe repair shop—was the perfect setup and that was his goal—"

"Minus your parents' poor health, he was inviting you to have the same life you had."

"Except without the feelings my parents had for each other—I liked Trip, but that was as far as it went. And I wanted to go to college, and he didn't want me to do that, so there was no way I was marrying him."

"And the second guy?"

"I dated him in college. Lou. His family owns a factory that manufactures and sells some sort of cog that almost every piece of machinery uses. When he finished college he was set to be trained to take over for his father to run things—"

"Another bigwig?"

"Not on the level of the Rumsons, but Lou's family is definitely well-off, so yes, I guess you could say he was another bigwig-in-the-making at least."

"Offering another bigger life."

"In Texas."

"But your family needed you in Billings so you said no?" Dag guessed.

"My family needed me in Billings *and* I also didn't have strong enough feelings for Lou to marry him— same as you and the contortionist."

"The contortionist wasn't one of my two other serious relationships. I told you that didn't go anywhere."

Shannon merely smiled. She'd just been giving him a hard time.

She finished her wine then and did a sit-up to put her glass on the coffee table before settling comfortably back alongside Dag again.

He did the same thing but when he sat back he turned slightly to his side so he could look at her. He also stretched an arm along the sofa behind her head.

"So let me see if I have this straight. Three proposals—two of them offering bigger lives—but what made you turn them all down was—"

"The same thing that made you turn down the two women you dated for long periods of time but didn't want to make a commitment to—the way I felt about them. Or, actually, the way I *didn't* feel about them. There was nothing really *wrong* with any of them. But with every one of them, if I went a week or two without seeing them, I was okay with it."

And yet with Dag she didn't seem to be okay with even a few hours without seeing him or talking to him…

She couldn't let that mean anything, she told herself.

"And the bottom line," Dag summarized, "is that bigger life or not—in any form—you won't accept less than what your folks had together."

Shannon shrugged. "My parents truly, truly loved each other. And as sappy as it may sound, after seeing that, after witnessing with my own two eyes that that kind of love does exist, it's something I have to hold out for."

Dag nodded his understanding but Shannon had the impression that there was something he wanted to say yet wasn't.

"What?" she asked. "You don't believe that kind of love exists?"

"I'm just wondering…"

"About?"

"Well, we can't count the high school kid because he wasn't offering the feelings or a bigger life. But with the other two guys you haven't had much trouble turning down the bigger life because the feelings weren't there. What happens if the feelings come without the bigger life?"

How had they gotten back on this subject she hadn't wanted to talk about?

"I don't know," she said. "But you're kind of harshing my buzz—"

Dag laughed again. "*That's* not what I had in mind!"

"I know. But here we are, with the Christmas tree and the fire and the wine and—"

"Maybe you'd rather hear more about the contortionist," he said, obviously getting the message. "Shall I tell you how she once got me out of a speeding ticket by dislocating her toes and telling the cop I was rushing her to the hospital because she'd broken her foot?"

"Oh, no! Stop!" Shannon said in horror, closing her eyes as if to block out the vision.

When she opened them again it was to Dag studying her and smiling a small, secret smile. Then he said, "What does it mean if I hate not seeing you for even a few hours?" he asked then, echoing her own thought of moments earlier.

"That you're really, really bored and need a hobby?"

He shook his handsome head as if he'd considered that, but then he said, "Nope, I don't think so...."

She knew that her own craving to be with him didn't come out of boredom, either, but she was afraid to think about what it might mean that every minute she was away from him was spent wishing she wasn't.

Then he came nearer and kissed her. And she recognized one of the reasons she craved being with him— because for the second time, the moment their lips met she felt an overwhelming sense of well-being, of euphoria, of just plain gladness that still didn't dampen the sheer excitement that kissing him flooded her with.

Shannon raised a hand to the side of his chiseled face as she answered his kiss, parting her lips, kissing him in return, welcoming his tongue when it came.

He was braced on his side, on one elbow, but with that hand he took hers where it rested on the sofa cushion, holding it while he wrapped his other arm around her and turned her more toward him.

And while Shannon knew it was probably not wise, her knee bent and her leg drifted over his.

That definitely lit a match to the kiss—mouths opened wider and tongues played with more fervor, more daring and audacity.

Shannon's hand went from the side of Dag's face along the unyielding column of his neck to his shoulder, to his chest, encased in the waffly weave of that thermal shirt.

Had his nipple grown slightly hard at her touch? The idea made her smile inside. And it made her own nipples tighten into much more adept little knots in memory of his hands on them last night. His mouth…

And if her own mouth opened a bit wider beneath his at just that thought? If her tongue met his more boldly? If a new hunger erupted in that kiss? She couldn't help it.

Not that Dag seemed to mind—he gave as good as he got in the joust they were toying at, and then he did her one better still, and brought his hand from her back to the side of her waist where it took nothing to find his way under that short sweater to bare skin.

His hand was warm, slightly calloused, so, so strong. He did a light massage of her side, racking her with memories of what he could do to more sensitive parts of her. Parts of her that were straining against her bra, her sweater, pining for his attention.

She demonstrated, pressing her fingers into his pectoral, releasing only to press again, inspiring a throaty chuckle from him.

Then his tongue changed to playful, instigating a little cat and mouse before he ended that kiss altogether and said, "I can't go home in the state I was in last night."

Her own unmet yearnings of the previous evening had been all she'd thought about. She hadn't considered what condition he might have been left in.

But now here they were again, and the choice was clear-cut—either they stopped before this went any further, or they didn't stop at all....

And stopping the previous evening had been bad enough.

Shannon kissed him again, a long, lingering, sensuous-but-not-sexy kiss, while her mind spun.

Before, she'd been worried and unsettled by the primal, out-of-control side he'd unveiled in her. The side that she could feel fighting to be unleashed again.

Before, she'd found willpower in reminding herself that they wanted different things.

But tonight...

Tonight she couldn't find the inclination to summon any kind of control.

Tonight she just kept kissing him and thinking that this wasn't her entire future or her whole life. That it wasn't his entire future or his whole life, either. That this was just now. One night. Christmastime. With a man who made her feel things she'd never felt before. Things she didn't want to leave behind without exploring them all...

"Maybe you just shouldn't go home..." she whispered

in a moment's pause between kissing him and having him kiss her back—but with some reserve. A reserve that remained even as she felt his lips stretch into a smile.

Then his head reared away from that kiss altogether and he peered down into her eyes. "Are you sure about that?" he asked skeptically in a low, husky voice.

"I am," she confirmed, rubbing her foot against his calf.

Dag continued to study her, to read her expression as if real assurance could only be there.

And maybe he found what he was looking for, because after a moment he smiled a small smile and said, "And Rumson—you're sure you're done with him? It's over? Finished? History for you?"

"All of that."

He did more looking into her eyes, more of what she thought of as soul-searching, although it seemed as if it wasn't so much her soul he was searching now, but his own.

After another moment his smile grew and turned devilish. "If you change your mind, I'm gonna have to run naked through the snow to cool off."

She wanted him naked all right, but not in the snow....

And her answer was to pull free the back half of his shirttails from his waistband and kiss him again, marveling at just how far her newly discovered wild side would go. Because she'd never taken any steps whatsoever to seduce another man and yet here she was...

With her thigh riding higher and higher on Dag's...

He was returning her kiss again but still cautiously. At least for a few minutes—maybe while he made up his own mind about the wisdom in this.

But then his mouth opened wide over hers once more,

his tongue reclaimed hers with a vengeance, and that hand at her side went straight up to cup her breast, sending a tingle of delight to skitter across the surface of her skin.

That was when inhibitions flew out the window.

Shannon yanked the remainder of his shirt from his jeans and both of her hands crawled up the widening expanse of his back, pressing her palms to follow the highs and lows of muscle and bone and sinew.

When she reached his shoulders he broke away from kissing her long enough for her to pull his shirt off, and for one brief moment before he returned to that kiss, she got to see the glory that was a professional athlete's shoulders and biceps and broad, broad chest.

And even when he'd blocked her view, even when he'd drawn her into another wildly wet and wicked kiss, she could still run her hands all over that naked torso, glorying in the feel.

She hadn't had quite enough of that when, without warning, Dag tore his mouth from hers to do a quick repositioning that turned him to lie flat on his back on the sofa, lifting Shannon to sit atop him, straddling that portion of him that had apparently caused him problems last night and tonight offered only promise.

He unfastened the buttons of her sweater while she feasted on her second view of his bare chest and flat, honed stomach, running her hands from its center to his sides to absorb the sight and feel of him all at once, provoking him to arch his waist off the couch just enough that the hard ridge of him tantalized her even further.

Then off came her sweater, leaving her lacy, demi-cup bra and the upper swell of her breasts exposed to him.

She thought she would feel more shy than she did at that first loss of her own clothes but instead that wilder side took over once again. She basked in the heat of his dark eyes as they took their turn at feasting on her with an appreciation that brought a smile to his oh-so-ruggedly-handsome face.

But looking wasn't nearly as good as touching and with a little laugh, Dag pulled her down to kiss her again, rolling them both to their sides.

Somewhere along the way her bra had come unhooked and he tossed that aside, as well, giving himself free access. Free access that he used to best advantage as one mighty hand closed around her now-naked breast, kneading, caressing, massaging, causing a fresh wave of desire to erupt in her that was relayed in the pinpoint pebble her nipple became in his palm.

But last night there had been even more…

Even better…

And when his mouth abandoned hers so he could kiss a moist trail downward to take her breast that way again, she couldn't keep from greeting him with an arch of her spine and a soft moan.

Circling, flicking, nipping at her. Teasing her nipple with the faint tip of his tongue. Sucking hard, then soft, he brought things to life in her that were sweeter and more intense than she'd ever known.

His hands went to the button on her jeans, opening that, too, unzipping the zipper. He pulled her pants off, taking her stockings with them, while his tongue twirled around the outer edge of her navel, before his mouth found her other breast and occupied it with the same wonders.

That was when it occurred to her that she could have more of him, too. That his jeans could go the same way hers had.

She reached for his waistband button, finding so much

more than she'd bargained for in the burgeoning behind that zipper that almost parted on its own when the button was undone.

With a little help from him, off went his jeans and socks, as well, and then he clasped her rear end in one hand big enough to cradle it and pulled her tight up against him.

But not so tight that she couldn't fit her hand between them to find that steely shaft and enclose it in her grip to make him groan with pleasure and pulse into her palm.

He abandoned her breast again and rediscovered her mouth with his, kissing her with a wide-open, seeking kiss as he shed her lacy panties.

Then he reached to the floor, fumbling among their discarded clothes until he found his jeans and took protection from his pocket. He returned to kissing her with a sexy playfulness while he put on the condom.

Once he had, he was moving her again. This time to lie on her back so he could come over her, between her legs that parted in invitation.

But it was more kisses that came first. Beginning at her knees, going up one thigh. He dropped a kiss at a spot just below her belly button and proceeded to leave a trail of them up her middle to her breasts again.

One after the other, he drew her straining, arousal-engorged breasts into his mouth, flicking his tongue to her nipples, using tender teeth to drive her to the brink of insanity with wanting so much more that she would be writhing beneath him.

And when she was, the body kisses began again, this time traveling up her breastbone to her throat, to her chin, to her mouth...

And at the same moment his tongue made an

impertinent entrance, he slid into her down below, too, in one smooth movement that joined them as if there were no other, more perfect fit.

Shannon's body answered all on its own. Her spine arched from its lowest point, pulling her shoulders, her neck off the sofa in turn, before the full ripple washed through her and the pure force of having him inside her became a reality.

An incredible reality...

Only then did he begin to move—slowly at first, making it easy for her to follow his lead, building desire, anticipation, increasing speed and intensity until their mouths separated and just their bodies moved in perfect rhythm, perfect harmony, perfect communication. Faster and faster. Shannon clung to Dag's massive shoulders. His big hands were on either side of her head. His long, strong arms braced him above her. And with each thrust of his hips, each meeting of hers to his, each pitch that took him to the very core of her, passion mounted and grew. And grew...

Until things sprang to life in her that had never known life before, taking over, taking *her* over, embracing her to lift her higher and higher and higher still.

She could feel her own heartbeat racing. She could feel the power and strength in every muscle of Dag's body. She watched his own passion mounting in the tense lines of his sexy, sexy face until she couldn't keep her eyes open to see it as she reached that peak he was taking her to, a peak better than she'd known was possible. A peak that held her in an explosion of ecstasy that she'd never experienced the same way, with the same astounding, astonishing, breathtaking splendor that seemed to freeze her in time and space for that one blissful moment...

That one blissful moment that Dag suddenly burst

into himself, plunging so deeply into her that it was more than a meeting, a matching, it was a union, a melding together of spirits and souls, a bonding that Shannon had also never experienced, that left her not only spent, not only satisfied and satiated, but a little dazed and dumbfounded by just how profound it had been...

Then Dag lowered himself to lie fully atop her, to kiss the side of her neck, to breathe warmth there and bring her back to earth, to herself, to a place where she could catch her own breath and tell herself it had just been some phenomenon of rapture...

"Wow..." Dag whispered in awe.

"Wow..." Shannon echoed the word and the sentiment.

"That was something..."

Something she still couldn't fully fathom.

And maybe neither could he because for a brief while they just stayed the way they were, basking in the afterglow before he slipped out of her, rolled to his side and half covered her with his big body while he insinuated one arm under her, wrapped the other over her, and held her to him.

"Tell me I didn't hurt you," he asked then.

"You didn't," she answered, looking up at him, savoring the sight of his hair mussed more than usual, of the tiny lines that formed around the corners of his mouth when he smiled. A smile so sweet she couldn't keep from raising a hand to his cheek.

"Now tell me you want me to stay the night," he commanded.

"I want you to stay the night." She had no problem saying it because she couldn't imagine having him get up, dress and go. She couldn't imagine losing the warmth of his amazing body and getting into her bed tonight without him.

But now that neither of them was going to have to face that, Dag settled his chin on top of her head. She could feel fatigue weighing him down as he muttered, "Good. So good…and if you give me just a catnap, it can be good again…" he tantalized.

Shannon nuzzled into his neck and closed her eyes. "I guess we'll see," she taunted him.

"Oh, yeah, we'll see all right," he said as if he were accepting the challenge.

But accepting it or not, the arm that was across her stomach suddenly became slack enough to let her know that he'd fallen asleep, and Shannon closed her eyes, too.

She was warm and oh-so-comfortable there on the sofa, with Dag's big body partially her blanket, the fire still roaring and the Christmas lights shining down on them.

And in that moment that had its own special kind of perfection, she fell asleep, too.

Chapter Twelve

Every Christmas Eve, Northbridge held a non-denominational service at the church followed by a potluck supper in the church basement. Year after year, much of the town chose to spend that evening dressed in their finest, attending the event with their whole family. This year the Mackeys and the McKendricks planned to be among them.

To Dag that meant that he was going to be with Shannon again. But in advance of that, he slipped out of her apartment well before dawn and went to his house to work all day.

Had it been up to him, he would have spent the day the way he'd spent the previous night—with Shannon, making love, napping, making love again and again and again.

But he'd also seen the merit to Shannon's wish to keep things private. So it wasn't until everyone was dressed and ready to leave for the Christmas Eve service that evening that he saw her again. And by then it had already been arranged that she would drive into town with Hadley, Chase and Cody.

Saying that he wanted his own vehicle at the church to allow himself the freedom to leave whenever he chose, Dag was left to follow behind Chase's car, watching Shannon through his windshield.

At the church they all filed into a pew—with Shannon separated from him by Chase and Hadley—and the most Dag could do was steal a few glimpses of Shannon during the service.

The service that spoke of gratitude and caused Dag to think how grateful he was to have met Shannon, to have had the night together that they'd had.

The service that spoke of counting blessings and making the best of every gift, and also brought Shannon to Dag's mind.

The service that spoke of rejoicing and celebrating and holding close what was most dear—and again it was only Shannon who Dag could think of in those terms.

When the service was over, they went into the church basement where there were so many people that Dag still didn't get a minute alone with Shannon. A minute to pull her into his arms the way he was itching to. To kiss her, to feel her body against his like he had so many times last night.

And now that the meal was finished, while everyone else mingled, Dag was sitting alone at the cafeteria table, nursing a glass of eggnog and watching Shannon.

Three-year-old Tia had taken her to the Christmas tree to show her the ornaments that Tia's preschool class had made. But when desserts were laid out on the buffet table, Tia abandoned Shannon to an elderly couple who

Dag thought were likely talking to her about her late grandmother.

And all Dag could think was how beautiful Shannon was and that he wanted her so much it was almost driving him out of his mind…

She'd twisted her hair into a knot at the crown of her head and left the ends of it to spring out like a geyser. She was wearing a simple, long-sleeved white mohair knit dress that skimmed her curves and wrapped the column of her neck in a high-standing turtleneck. The hem of her dress ended just above her knees and from there Dag's gaze followed shapely legs to the three-inch high heels that he couldn't help picturing her wearing with nothing else at all—something he thought he might be able to persuade her to actually do now that he'd discovered a hint of a daring streak in her. A hint of a daring streak that he took great pleasure in bringing out in her.

But then there were so many things he took great pleasure in bringing out in her. So many things he just took pleasure in when he was with her.

Everything, in fact…

Gratitude and counting blessings and cherishing gifts and rejoicing and celebrating and holding close what was most dear…

The sentiments of the service came back to him then, making him recall that it had been Shannon he'd counted as a blessing, Shannon he'd been grateful for, cherished and rejoiced and celebrated in. Shannon he'd mentally held close and dear…

And it struck him that the things he'd felt making love to Shannon had been unlike anything he'd ever come across with anyone else. What he'd felt since then, what he'd felt all through the church service, what he felt at that moment, wasn't anything he'd ever felt before, either. Not even with Sandra. Not with anyone.

But the day after Christmas, Shannon was leaving...

And suddenly that became an unbearable thought.

How the hell had he come to that? he asked himself as it struck him just how unbearable a thought her leaving was. How had he gone from believing she was engaged, from knowing to steer clear of her not only because of the other guy in her life but also because she wanted bigger and better things than he could offer, to this? To wanting her so much he would have gladly faced another five men—all of them with crowbars this time—if it meant he could end up with her?

Now *that* was crazy!

But somehow it was true.

And as that fact sunk in, Dag had to face it.

He wanted Shannon Duffy.

And not just in bed.

He wanted Shannon Duffy in his life. Constantly and continuously. Permanently. In his life, by his side, as close as he could get her every minute from now until the end of time...

That beautiful woman in white...

Who was more recently out of a relationship with another man than Sandra had been—a man Sandra had ended up with after all.

That beautiful woman in white who wanted a bigger life—much like his mother had always wanted more...

Maybe I'm just the dumbest idiot who ever lived, he thought as he reminded himself of the two reasons he'd known from the beginning not to get involved with Shannon.

Two penalties, he told himself, in a game he swore had to be squeaky-clean for him to ever play again...

And yet something caused him to balk at thinking of Shannon in terms of infractions—hockey or otherwise. Shannon was too good for that. She was generous and kind and funny and sweet and caring.

Did she want a life that had more to offer than she'd known growing up? Than she'd known through the course of taking care of ailing parents?

She did, but Dag understood that. And he couldn't fault her for it. He'd wanted to play hockey and he hadn't let anything hold him back. Good parents or not, Shannon could well have done the same thing. But she hadn't. And now that she was free to do more, to have more of the kind of life she wanted? He couldn't hold it against her that she was determined to do that.

Plus there wasn't anything in what she wanted, anything about Shannon that was really like his mother—it wasn't as if Shannon put on airs or thought she was better than anyone, she just wanted a bigger bite of life. And he thought she deserved that. If anyone deserved that, it was someone who had done as much caring for and sacrificing for other people as Shannon had.

But if he thought that she deserved a bigger bite of life, he couldn't be the one to ask her not to take it, he told himself.

Because that's what it would cost her if he tried to keep her by his side, in his life, as close as he could get her every minute until the end of time.

It meant asking her to sacrifice what she wanted again.

Unless he did the sacrificing...

It took him a moment to accept that as potentially another way to go. And another, longer moment to consider it.

He could change his own course for her...

Surprisingly, that wasn't so difficult a thing to imagine once it had occurred to him. It was a lot easier to think about that than about her walking away the day after tomorrow and his never seeing her again.

But here he was, thinking about throwing his own plans out the window, about making a significant—a *huge*—alteration in his own life, without knowing how she felt.

And that was a very big deal.

Because it was the feelings that really mattered, he reminded himself. Shannon had turned down three proposals because her feelings for those other guys weren't strong enough, because they hadn't matched up to what her parents had felt for each other. If she wasn't feeling anything for him that was as strong as what he was feeling for her...

Dag stalled. He couldn't think beyond that.

He couldn't entertain *any* thought beyond that one, now that that one had come into his head—*did* Shannon have feelings for him? And if she did, were they the kind of feelings he had for her? The kind her parents had shared that had made them content to live any sort of life as long as they lived it together?

Until he knew what was going on with Shannon, where he stood, everything else was inconsequential. He *had* to know....

And he had to know now!

He got up from the table and crossed the room to her, grateful that when he reached her the conversation she was having with the elderly couple was ending with them wishing her a merry Christmas and moving on.

Grateful, too, that when she saw him, when her luminous blue-green eyes met his, her expression seemed to light up.

"Any chance we might slip out of here?" he asked without segue.

Shannon seemed more intrigued than surprised by that idea—which he was glad to see. "Think anyone will notice?" she asked.

"I don't care if they do," he confessed, hearing the note of urgency in his own voice but not caring about that, either.

"Okay," Shannon said with a smile he'd seen several times the night before, a smile that let him know she thought it was something other than talk that he had in mind for them.

But if all went well, talking could only be the beginning, so he didn't elaborate. Instead he nodded in the direction of the doors and that was where they went.

No one noticed them as Dag helped Shannon on with her coat, threw his on, too, and then ushered her out into the cold where a light, fluffy snow had started to fall.

He was parked in a nearby spot in the church lot and they hurried to it.

"This was a long day," Shannon said as he held the passenger door open for her and helped her into the truck.

"Way, way too long," he agreed emphatically, not sure she meant what he did—that the day had dragged by because he hadn't been with her...

Once Shannon was settled, he shut the door and rushed around the front end of the truck, nearly bounding behind the wheel and starting the engine. Then he put it into gear and headed out, deciding as he did that he wasn't going to beat around the bush.

So, with a glance in her direction, he said, "I missed you so much today that I screwed up everything I tried to do. I nearly ran into the back of Chase's car tonight following you here because I was looking at you instead of the taillights. I haven't been able to take my eyes off you all night and while I was doing that I figured something out. I figured out what I want for Christmas."

"I hope it's what I got you, because I don't think there's any twenty-four-hour shopping in Northbridge," Shannon joked.

But Dag merely looked over at her and said, "I want you, Shannon."

Her eyebrows formed two perfect arches over her eyes and he could see that she didn't know what to say. But that was okay. He'd known this would shock her. It shocked him. But that didn't deter him. In fact he liked that he knew her well enough already to have predicted this response and it just made him smile.

"How long did your parents know each other before they realized what they had together?" he asked.

"My father said it was love-at-first-sight for him. My mother said it took her ten or fifteen minutes. But I think that was a joke…"

"Maybe it wasn't…"

Dag had to look back at the road, but he went on talking. "Here's how it is for me—I love Northbridge, I really do. I love Northbridge as much as I loved hockey. Knowing the end of my career would put me back here was the only thing that got me through. But now there's you and I have to tell you that when I think about being anywhere in the world—including Northbridge—*without* you, it isn't where I want to be."

Another glance at her showed him the perplexed expression on her face, but still he was undaunted.

"What we've had since we met hasn't been like anything I've ever had with anyone else—there's never been this kind of instant connection, as if I've stumbled into the one person I was honestly intended to be with. You know what you said about the guys in your life? About how part of what told you they were wrong for you was that you didn't care when you *didn't* see them?"

"I remember..."

"Well, I never realized it before, but the same has been true for me with every other woman in my life. Until you."

He had to brake for a stop sign and, despite the fact that there wasn't any traffic to keep him there, he stayed so he could look at her again to say, "I wasn't kidding when I said I hate not seeing you for even an hour—I *hate* it. There's never been this... I'm not even sure how to put it... This feeling like nothing really matters unless I'm doing it with you. Or for you. And then there was last night...last night was off the Richter scale."

He watched her smile just barely, as if the memory of their night together was so remarkable for her, too, that she couldn't help it. And that gave him the courage to say, "I think it's been the same for you..."

He finally drove on, giving her a moment to tell him that he was wrong, that she didn't have feelings that were anything like what he was describing.

But instead, in a quiet voice, she said, "It has been different for me than anything has ever been with anyone else. But—"

"I know," he said to stop her, guessing what she was going to say. "You want a bigger life than Northbridge has to offer. And you should have it. So I've been thinking, and if you want to be the first woman on Mars, I'm willing to be the first man—if that's what it takes to be with you. If you decide to invest in your friend's school and live and work in Beverly Hills, I'll see if I can coach hockey somewhere there—"

"You just bought my grandmother's house!"

"And I'll turn around and sell it. The point is, Shannon, what I realized tonight is that the only thing that matters to me—that truly matters—is that I want you. I want to be with you. I want to live whatever kind of life makes you happy, because the only thing that's going to make me honestly, genuinely happy, too, is you. Anywhere. Living with wild monkeys, if that's what you want. As long as I'm with you…"

The words were hanging in the air as Dag turned onto the road that led to Logan and Meg's place. But that was when both Dag and Shannon spotted a black limousine up ahead, already parked beside the big farmhouse. A black limousine that certainly didn't belong there. And abruptly put everything else on hold.

Dag hit the brakes purely out of reflex, knowing instantly that there was only one person who was likely to have come to Northbridge in a limousine on Christmas Eve.

"That can't be…" he muttered darkly to himself.

"Wes," Shannon said, giving voice to Dag's worst thoughts.

Wes Rumson.

In what Dag had no doubt was a grand gesture.

And even if this one didn't come with a crowbar, Dag thought it couldn't have hit him any harder.

The other guy from Shannon's so-recent past.

The guy Shannon had said she was finished with.

And Dag couldn't help wondering if it was possible that he'd made the same mistake twice—that Shannon wasn't as finished with Rumson as she'd said. That a grand gesture from the rich politician might sway her still…

"Can I turn us around and go the other way?" Dag joked feebly.

"If it's Wes, I'll have to see him."

"*If?* Who else is it gonna be?"

And what else is the politician going to do but pull out all the stops to get you to say you'll marry him...

Dag really was tempted to jam his truck into Reverse and back the hell out of that drive. Sweep Shannon away. Make *that* grand gesture.

But he resisted the urge, knowing if she was determined to hear out the other guy, there was no stopping it.

He took his foot off the brake and went the rest of the way up the drive, reaching the limo right about the time Wes Rumson got out the back of it—tall and straight, dressed in a suit and tie underneath a custom-tailored overcoat, looking as if he were ready to take the governor's chair right then.

Dag pulled to a second stop beside him and Shannon rolled down her window.

"What are you doing here, Wes?" she asked, not sounding thrilled to see him, but also not perturbed or angry—the way Dag would have preferred. And probably not knowing that that alone was like a sucker punch.

"I came to talk to you," the politician said as if he'd just driven around the block rather than from his family's estate in Billings.

Shannon didn't jump at that and Dag took some comfort in what he interpreted as hesitancy. But then she said, "I'm staying in the apartment around back. You can follow us."

"Right behind you," Wes Rumson said as if it had been an engraved invitation he was expecting and entitled to. Then he ducked into the limo's rear seat and Shannon rolled up the window again.

And Dag just sat there, fighting so many inclinations that he knew he couldn't act on.

But Shannon was looking at him again, her brow furrowed once more, and rather than reassuring him, she said a simple, "I'm sorry."

That Rumson is here? That you're dropping me flat to talk to him? Or that you can't say yes to me, either...

Dag didn't know. And there was no time to ask. And even if there was, was this really the best moment to force her into a corner?

Dag knew it wasn't, so he merely raised his chin in answer to her apology—whatever it was for—and drove around to the garage, followed by that damn black limousine.

Without another word, Shannon got out of the truck at the foot of the apartment steps, and Dag watched her lead the politician up those same stairs he'd been climbing with her every other night. The politician—the man—who wanted her, too. Who could offer her more than he could. Who she must have had feelings for in one way or another. Who she might still have feelings enough for to take what he was offering after all...

And that was when Dag felt something that hit him harder than any beating he'd ever taken. On the ice or off.

Dazed and confused—that was how Shannon felt as she turned on the apartment's lights and took off her coat. First there had been all that Dag had stunned her by saying. Now Wes. She was having trouble gathering her wits.

But Wes was standing just inside the door, taking off

his own coat as if she'd asked him to, and she had to deal with him. So she pushed aside what Dag had said and turned to face her former non-fiancé.

"It's Christmas Eve and you drove all the way to Northbridge?" she said when Wes hadn't taken the lead.

"I wanted to see you. To talk to you."

"And you had Herbert drive you? Didn't he want to be with his family—his *kids*—tonight?"

"I'm paying him well. If I'd driven myself I would have wasted the time. Instead I was able to work on my next speech while he drove—that is his job."

Shannon was thinking about the three kids the driver had shown her pictures of and of them not having their father with them tonight of all nights because Wes's work came first. For Wes at least.

Not to mention that even as he'd been coming to see her, she hadn't been what he was actually focusing on.

"I'm still not sure why you're here, Wes," Shannon said.

The tall, impressive politician stepped nearer and took a velvet ring box from his pocket. "I thought maybe a private Christmas Eve proposal might be welcomed with a little more favor," he said, opening the box to reveal the biggest diamond Shannon had ever seen.

But even dazzled by the diamond, Shannon thought that this was nothing but another tack he was taking. A retry that had the earmarks of a new strategy he and his cousin had devised.

Or maybe coming after what Dag had just said to her—full of so much emotion, so much passion—this just sounded rehearsed and superficial. Either way, it wouldn't have swayed her even before all that Dag had said on the drive home.

She shook her head, wondering how many times she was going to have to turn this man down to get him to accept that she wouldn't marry him. "The *way* you propose, the timing, whether it's public or private—those aren't the reasons I won't marry you, Wes. I told you—"

"Yes, you did tell me. But I think you're mistaken, Shannon. We may not have the mirror image of what your parents had, but we're not so bad together. I know people who have much less to build on than we do and they make perfectly successful pairings. We get along, we can always find something to talk about, we have things in common, we both want to make our mark—"

"You want to make your mark. I just want—"

"I know what you want. But how much bigger can your life be than as the wife of the governor? As maybe the wife of a president some day? And you can make your mark, too. You can push education—*I'll* push education, it's a popular topic and with you being a teacher, you can do great things for the state, for the country. We make a good team."

"And you love me so much you can't live without me," she said facetiously, as if she were feeding him the line he should have used.

"I do love you, Shannon," he contended. "You know that. Maybe not the way you think your father loved your mother—"

"It isn't something *I think,* it's something I know."

"Still, I care for you. The same way any normal husband cares for his wife. We could have a lifelong, fruitful marriage. Kids. And you'd never again have to spend a Christmas Eve, a Christmas, alone like this, without family."

"That's why you're really here now, isn't it?" Shannon

said as it dawned on her. "You came because you thought I'd be at a particularly low point tonight, tomorrow. That I'd be vulnerable…" Not because he wanted to make this first holiday after the loss of her family easier for her, not because he wanted to make sure she was all right. But to use what he'd hoped might be a weak moment to his own advantage.

She considered telling him just how not-alone she'd been since arriving in Northbridge, or tonight, how not-alone she would be tomorrow with Chase and Hadley and Cody and Meg and Logan and Tia. And Dag… But it didn't seem worth it, so she merely repeated, "No, Wes, I won't marry you."

"I just don't understand you, Shannon," he said curtly, sounding frustrated and aggravated that this play still hadn't accomplished his goal. "We've been involved for a long time. We've talked about marriage. Your parents are gone so there's not that holding you back. You've said you want more out of life and I'm here offering that. Get your head out of the clouds and let's be realistic—you idealized your parents' relationship. You made it some sort of storybook love that nothing can live up to—"

"In all the time we've known each other, Wes, you only met my parents twice. You don't know what kind of relationship they had."

And Shannon knew that he was right when he'd said he didn't understand her because he genuinely didn't. He didn't understand why there was absolutely no temptation, no appeal in this passionless *Bigger Life* that he was offering.

But she wasn't even slightly tempted by it. Despite the fact that he was Wes Rumson, that he was impeccably dressed, handsome, cultured, intelligent, wealthy, well respected. Despite the fact that they *had* had a pleasant-enough, enjoyable-enough relationship that had met some of her needs.

It just didn't matter to her because she hadn't had even the tiniest thrill when she'd first seen his limousine, the tiniest thrill at thinking that he'd come all the way from Billings on Christmas Eve just for her. She certainly didn't want to run into his arms. She wasn't aching to have him touch her, kiss her—everything that came instantly with every thought, every glimpse of Dag.

Dag, whom she'd had to leave hanging…

"Go home, Wes," she advised then. "Go back to Billings to be with your own family, let Herbert get to his. This—you and I—just wasn't meant to be. I might vote for you, but I won't marry you."

Wes snapped closed the ring box like the jaws of an alligator and put it back in his jacket pocket. "I don't think you know what you want."

He was right about that, too, because it wasn't as if she was ready to rush to Dag and accept all he'd laid out for her either…

"But I know what I *don't* want," she said quietly.

Wes remained with his pale brown eyes boring into her from beneath a fierce frown, shaking his head. Then he put his coat back on, all the while watching her as if he thought she'd gone out of her mind.

"Once I announce this publicly we're through—you know that?" he warned. "The polls may like you now, but yo-yoing would cost me votes."

And she wasn't worth the loss to him.

"I know, Wes. Just make the announcement and get it over with."

"We could have had a good thing, Shannon. I hope you don't regret this."

"I'm sorry, Wes," was her only response, the second apology she'd made in the last half hour.

And it brought back to mind the first one she'd made as Wes cast her a final glare and walked out of the apartment—it brought Dag back to mind.

And all he'd said.

And all she really needed to think about.

Chapter Thirteen

Almost the moment that Wes Rumson was out of sight, he was out of Shannon's mind, replaced with thoughts of Dag. And the things Dag had been in the process of saying to her on the way home from the church.

Because those things had been monumental.

Dag was willing to give up everything for her....

She hadn't fully grasped it at the time but as she re-hashed it all in her head, she began to realize that that really was what he'd been saying. Offering.

He was willing to live any life she wanted to live. Anywhere. He was even willing to sell the house he'd just bought from her, to follow her to Beverly Hills, if she decided that was what she wanted.

Her grandmother had left her own life behind to help Shannon care for her parents. But other than that, no one else—certainly no man—had ever been willing to do anything that big for her. All three of the other men who had proposed to her had wanted her on their terms and their terms alone.

Because Dag had been so convincing, because his words had been so heartfelt, she didn't doubt that he'd meant what he'd said, that he *would* give up his house, Northbridge, his plans for his future, for her.

The way she knew her dad would have given up anything and everything for her mom...

And after Wes had stood there only moments before, basically telling her that she was a dreamer to think she could ever find something like that, that she should just settle and accept what Wes believed most people had, Dag's sacrifice stood out as even greater.

But he hadn't said it was any sacrifice at all. Dag had said only that he was willing to do whatever it took to be with her because she was what he wanted.

Which *was* the way her parents had felt.

And maybe it was time to stop ignoring her own feelings, she told herself. To stop locking them up and keeping them at bay, stop telling herself that everything that was going on with Dag was a lark, and take a look at what she actually did feel for him.

Realizing she was still standing in the middle of the living room, Shannon went to sit down. She looked at the sofa, at the floor between the sofa and the fireplace. At the hearth. At the spots where she and Dag had ended up so many evenings since they'd met. Talking. Joking. Laughing. Kissing. Making love...

Seeing it all in her mind somehow helped to set free her feelings for him. To experience them with a clear head rather than in the uncontrollable bursts that had come in the heat of the moment. Uncontrollable bursts that she'd followed by hiding those feelings from herself again as soon as she could get them back under control.

And the power of those feelings was a little startling when they washed over her unrestricted, and undistracted.

Yes, she'd been aware of the fact that every minute she hadn't been with him she'd been thinking about him, watching the clock, counting the hours that would have to pass before she could see him again and wishing the time would go faster.

Yes, she'd been aware of a sense of contentment, of completion, of safety and security whenever she'd been with him.

Yes, she'd been aware that everything she'd done, everything she'd experienced, every food she'd eaten, every Christmas song she'd heard when she was with him had seemed to have a special, improved quality to it.

Yes, she'd been aware that she'd just felt happier whenever she was with him. Happier than she ever remembered feeling before. That she'd even been able to deal better with the moments when grief had paid her a return visit, she'd been able to talk about her parents and her grandmother with Dag without feeling as devastated by the loss. She'd been able to visit her grandmother's house and remember mainly good things.

But for some reason she hadn't associated any of that with having *feelings* for Dag.

And now she knew that—of course—that was where it had all come from.

Knowing that now, when she thought again about what he'd said on the way home, she suddenly couldn't deny that she felt all the same things he'd said he felt. That nothing seemed more important than being with him. That anything and everything seemed more manageable if she had him by her side. That there wasn't a single thing she could think of that she didn't want to share with him.

The way her parents had felt about each other...

Her jaw actually dropped a little when that struck her.

Was it possible that she actually *had* found with Dag what her parents had had?

Maybe a small part of her had worried that what Wes had said tonight might be true—that she was searching for, holding out for, something unrealistic or idealized. Or at least, unattainable. But suddenly she knew that wasn't true. Because what she felt for Dag was exactly what she'd seen in her parents' feelings for each other. It *did* exist. And she was in the throes of it.

She was in the throes of it so firmly, so deeply, so intensely that she understood Dag's willingness to give up Northbridge, his house, his plans, to be with her.

The problem was, she was too firmly, too deeply, too intensely in the throes of it to feel as if she could let him do that...

But if she didn't?

If she said yes to Dag but didn't let him give up everything for her, then she was saying yes to Northbridge, too. To living in her grandmother's house. To a life that might have more open air than an apartment over a shoe repair shop, but that would be lived in a place that wasn't even as big as Billings.

She'd be saying yes to a life that was, in some ways, even smaller than the life she'd known before.

And then what?

Would she end up feeling the way Dag's mother had? Isolated and unfulfilled and as if she was missing out?

That gave her some pause.

But then she began to think about Northbridge and what she'd discovered here. What she could have here over and above Dag.

She'd come to the small town feeling sad and alone, feeling disconnected. But all of that had gone away, because while Northbridge might not be large, it still had so much to offer. Such warm and caring and kind and fun-loving people who had embraced her, who had made her feel a part of things as well as a stronger connection with her grandmother's memory.

And in Northbridge she had a brother, a sister-in-law, a nephew. She had the beginnings of a tenuous relationship with her other two brothers. The thought of staying to cultivate all of that actually felt better to her than any of the thoughts she'd had about Beverly Hills, about risking her friendship with Dani by becoming business partners.

The plain truth, she finally realized, was exactly what Dag had said he felt about her. The most important thing to her was him. Being with him. But being with him in Northbridge had an appeal all its own and she knew deep down that she could be okay with that. With a lifetime of living here. If she always had Dag…

Which was what she suddenly knew without a doubt that she wanted. What she had to have. Right now!

But it hadn't been early when she and Dag had left the church. Topping that off with Wes's visit and then with all the thinking she'd just done since, and the evening was gone—it was very late and she knew that Dag couldn't be alone anymore, that Logan, Meg and Tia had to have come home a while ago.

She went to the window that looked onto the back of the main house. The room Dag was staying in faced the front, so she had no way of knowing if he was still awake or not, but in the rear of the house the only light on was in Meg and Logan's bedroom upstairs. And that went out a few seconds later, warning her that it was likely that by now everyone was in bed.

She hated that she'd left Dag the way she had, after the things he'd said to her, without anything but an apology for Wes's unwelcome appearance. And she couldn't imagine that Dag was thinking anything good or he would have been watching for Wes to leave and would have come to the apartment.

She could try his cell phone but she didn't want to do that. She wanted to see him. To see his face when she told him what she had to tell him. To have him wrap his arms around her and let her know he forgave her for running out on the most important thing he might ever have to say to her.

The doors to Logan and Meg's house all had keyless locks and she had the combination to the one on the back door—Meg had given it to her just in case she'd needed to get in at some point when they were gone. And even though Meg and Logan weren't gone, Shannon decided that she definitely needed to get in.

So without bothering with her coat, Shannon went out the apartment door, into the gently falling snow and across the yard.

The combination to the lock was easy and she punched it in quickly, instantly gaining access to the dark, silent house and feeling like a cat burglar as she went through the kitchen to the staircase that took her up to the bedrooms.

The bedrooms formed a semicircle around a large landing at the top of the stairs and Shannon forgot that there was a table just to the left of the steps. So when she turned in that direction she hit it, shoving it with a bang against the wooden railing.

She caught hold of it in a hurry to keep it from toppling over or making any more noise but apparently that had been noise enough, because just then from Tia's room came the three-year-old's voice.

"Santa?" she exclaimed.

In a panic, Shannon was about to dash back down the stairs to get out of sight when the door to the guest room opened. A surprised Dag registered that she was there, grabbed her wrist to pull her into his room, and—in his deep Santa voice—said, "Ho, ho, ho, little girls have to be asleep to get presents..."

Then he softly closed the door again.

He'd spun Shannon into the center of the bedroom and she watched him listen with his ear to the door for a moment to make sure his niece didn't take it any further. She couldn't help smiling at his quick thinking and impromptu acting. And at the sight of him shirtless, in a pair of sweatpants that dipped below his navel and made her shiver just a little with how sexy he looked.

But she wasn't sure if any of that was appropriate under the circumstances, so she forced a sober expression onto her face as Dag turned to her.

And the questioning challenge in his raised eyebrows let her know there were, indeed, more solemn things to deal with.

"I wondered if you were still here," he said.

"Where else would I be?"

"On your way to Christmas with the Rumsons?"

Shannon shook her head. "There was never a chance of that," she assured.

"There was if the guy had convinced you to marry him after all."

"There was never a chance of that, either. But at least I think Wes has accepted it now and he'll finally make the announcement that we aren't engaged." She paused a moment and then said, "Are you and I?"

That made Dag laugh involuntarily. And slightly forlornly. "Engaged? I don't know. I did a lot of talking. All I got from you was an *I'm sorry* before you hopped out of my truck to run off with that other guy."

"I don't remember any hopping or running," she pointed out.

"It must have just seemed like it to me."

"And you weren't even watching to see if I went off with him?"

"Couldn't. I knew I wouldn't be able to stand it if I had to see that."

"So you were just up here, going to bed?"

"I was just up here pacing and wondering and worrying and hating the hell out of the fact that there *was* another guy...."

"Maybe this time you should be glad there was," she told him then. "I've been comparing the two of you since we met. Not on purpose, it just seemed to keep happening. And Wes Rumson came up short every single time."

"Even with all the money and power and a *much* bigger life to offer you?"

"None of that matters. And neither do a lot of other things—like Beverly Hills..."

She watched his expression turn curious. And maybe cautiously optimistic. But before he could say anything she told him what she'd been thinking about since Wes had left tonight, the realizations she'd had, the decisions and conclusions she'd come to.

When she'd said her piece, she added, "So I don't know if what you were saying on the way home tonight was a proposal—"

"That's where it was headed. Number four for you."

"Well, I think this is the one I can say yes to...."

He frowned.

Shannon hadn't expected that and felt some uncertainty herself suddenly.

Then Dag said, "I just want to be clear—you're saying yes to me, but no to Beverly Hills with or without me?"

"I told you when we talked about it that I had my doubts. I've told Dani that. I still had doubts about it, even thinking that you would come with me, that I wouldn't be doing it alone. But Northbridge? It's sort of grown on me, and I don't have any doubts about living here, maybe teaching kindergarten here if I can...."

"And you're okay living in your grandmother's house?"

"We can make it our house, can't we?"

He finally smiled. "Yellow paint it is—warm and homey and sunny," he said, repeating her words from when she'd visited the house and they'd talked about whether he should paint the outside of the place white or return it to its original yellow.

And as if that settled everything, he pulled her into his arms then, kissing her the way she'd been craving to have him kiss her all day, all evening, certainly since finding him shirtless.

But the kiss didn't last long before he let go of her, yanked on a pullover hooded sweatshirt and then took her hand.

"Let's go where we don't have to worry about waking anybody," he suggested as he led her out of the guest room.

They moved quietly through the dark house—with Dag making one quick stop to snatch a present from under the tree—before they retraced Shannon's path to put them back at the apartment. There, Dag crossed his arms over his middle and instantly peeled off the sweatshirt.

And once he had, he pulled her to him again, kissing her a second time as if he'd been too long away from her lips.

Shannon had no resistance to him and let her hands do as they pleased, pressing to his naked chest, up and over his shoulders to his broad, hard back.

Everything else fell away then, along with Shannon's clothes and those sweatpants that Dag had on. Still kissing her, Dag picked her up and carried her to the bed where they made love with an urgency that said even mere hours of separation had been too much.

An urgency to reclaim what they'd discovered the night before, to stake a new and permanent claim now, with hands that caressed and teased and delighted, with mouths that clung together or broke apart to do amazing things elsewhere, with every inch of their bodies coming together as seamlessly as if one was split apart from the other long ago and had finally been reunited with its mate.

Together they reached an even more profound pinnacle that left Shannon drained and weak and limp in Dag's powerful arms as he rolled them both to their sides, cradling her, brushing her hair away from her face so he could look down into her eyes.

"I love you," he said then, for the first time.

"I love you, too," Shannon could answer without the slightest hesitancy. "With all my heart and soul."

"I want you to know that I won't let our life be small, even if we do live it here. I'll make sure it's a full one, and that you are always the biggest part of it for me—if that matters."

It mattered enough to bring moisture to her eyes that she had to blink back.

"We can still go to Beverly Hills, visit your friend, see her school, you know," he offered then, obviously again thinking of her, putting her ahead of himself.

"I'd like that. I'd like for Dani to meet you. And you to meet Dani."

"And if you change your mind and want to stay—"

"I won't," she said without the shadow of a doubt. "I really did fall in love with this place and the people here."

"Are you just using me to get your house back so you can move to Northbridge?" he joked.

"Yep," she answered glibly, tightening her muscles around him. "I'm just using you."

He slipped out of her then and left the bed long enough to retrieve the small package he'd taken from beneath Meg and Logan's tree.

Bringing it back, he kept hold of it until he was lying with Shannon beside him, in his arms again.

Only then did he hand it to her.

"Merry Christmas."

"You want me to open it now?"

"I do."

It wasn't easy in that position, but Shannon managed, opening a box that contained a very delicate chain.

"It's for your grandmother's ring," Dag explained. "You said—"

"That I would get a chain for it and wear it around my neck. And you remembered that?"

"It was part of what I went into town for yesterday."

She really did love this man....

"Thank you," Shannon said.

"Thank *you*."

"For?"

"For my Christmas gift."

"I haven't given it to you yet," she reminded, thinking of the cashmere sweater that was still under Meg and Logan's tree since that was where gift-opening was slated to occur in the morning.

"You gave me my gift," Dag insisted, taking the box that held the necklace and setting it on the nightstand. "I told you it was you I wanted."

"Oh, *that* Christmas gift," Shannon said. "I guess you're welcome, then."

"You don't ever have to give me anything else," he whispered in a husky voice. "Well, except maybe a couple of kids?"

"I can't promise them for Christmas, but I'll see what I can do."

He chuckled just a little, but Shannon saw his eyes drift closed as if they were too heavy to keep open, and she could feel him relaxing, falling asleep.

"I know—you need a nap," she said, guessing what he was about to tell her.

"Somebody kept me up almost the whole night last night."

"And you didn't get much sleep, either…"

He laughed, but he really was fading, and Shannon opted for giving in to her own fatigue.

She settled her head on his bare chest and closed her eyes, too, snuggling into Dag, knowing from the previous night that she would only nap for an hour or so before he would wake her with feathery kisses and everything would start again.

And just the prospect of that made her smile against him and marvel at how very, very much she loved him.

So much that she knew without question that living whatever kind of life, whatever size of life they ended up living, would be perfect as long as they were together.

Because now that her feelings for him were unbound, they were boundless, and that was what really mattered—not the life she led or where she led it, but who she got to share it with.

Just the way it had been for her parents.

Just the way she'd always wanted for herself.

And just what she'd found with Dag.

* * * * *

FINHAM LIBRARY

Cherish™

ROMANCE TO MELT THE HEART EVERY TIME

My wish list for next month's titles...

In stores from 16th November 2012:

❏ The Count's Christmas Baby – Rebecca Winters

& The Rancher's Unexpected Family – Myrna Mackenzie

❏ Snowed in at the Ranch – Cara Colter

& The Nanny Who Saved Christmas – Michelle Douglas

In stores from 7th December 2012:

❏ The English Lord's Secret Son – Margaret Way

& A Gift for All Seasons – Karen Templeton

❏ A Maverick for the Holidays – Leanne Banks

& A Maverick's Christmas Homecoming – Teresa Southwick

Available at WHSmith, Tesco, Asda, Eason, Amazon and Apple

Just can't wait?

Visit us Online

You can buy our books online a month before they hit the shops! **www.millsandboon.co.uk**

1112/2

Book of the Month

MICHELE HAUF
FOREVER WEREWOLF

nocturne™

MILLS & BOON

We love this book because...

Werewolves Trystan and Lexi's relationship comes under threat when he discovers a deadly secret about his heritage that could force him to choose between love and destiny in this thrilling paranormal romance.

On sale 16th November

Visit us Online

Find out more at
www.millsandboon.co.uk/BOTM

1112/BOTM

2 Free Books!

Join the Mills & Boon Book Club

Want to read more **Cherish**™ stories?
We're offering you **2 more**
absolutely **FREE!**

We'll also treat you to these fabulous extras:

- 🌹 **Books up to 2 months ahead of shops**

- 🌹 **FREE home delivery**

- 🌹 **Bonus books with our special rewards scheme**

- 🌹 **Exclusive offers… and much more!**

Treat yourself now!

Visit us Online

Get your FREE books now at
www.millsandboon.co.uk/freebookoffer

0712/S2YE

MILLS & BOON
Book Club

2 Free Books!

Get your free books now at
www.millsandboon.co.uk/freebookoffer

Or fill in the form below and post it back to us

THE MILLS & BOON® BOOK CLUB™—HERE'S HOW IT WORKS: Accepting your free books places you under no obligation to buy anything. You may keep the books and return the despatch note marked 'Cancel'. If we do not hear from you, about a month later we'll send you 5 brand-new stories from the Cherish™ series, including two 2-in-1 books priced at £5.49 each, and a single book priced at £3.49*. There is no extra charge for post and packaging. You may cancel at any time, otherwise we will send you 5 stories a month which you may purchase or return to us—the choice is yours. *Terms and prices subject to change without notice. Offer valid in UK only. Applicants must be 18 or over. Offer expires 31st January 2013. **For full terms and conditions, please go to www.millsandboon.co.uk/freebookoffer**

Mrs/Miss/Ms/Mr (please circle) _____

First Name _____

Surname _____

Address _____

_____ Postcode _____

E-mail _____

Send this completed page to: Mills & Boon Book Club, Free Book Offer, FREEPOST NAT 10298, Richmond, Surrey, TW9 1BR

Find out more at
www.millsandboon.co.uk/freebookoffer

Visit us Online

0712/S2YEA

& *Special Offers*

Every month we put together collections and longer reads written by your favourite authors.

Here are some of next month's highlights— and don't miss our fabulous discount online!

On sale 16th November   On sale 16th November   On sale 7th December

Save 20% *on all Special Releases*

Find out more at
www.millsandboon.co.uk/specialreleases

Visit us Online